FALL OF '33

ALSO BY GARY LEE ENTSMINGER &
SUSAN ELIZABETH ELLIOTT

Ophelia's Ghost (2008)

Remembering the Parables (2010)

Making the Most of WriteItNow 4 (2010)

Fall of '33

by

Gary Lee Entsminger

&

Susan Elizabeth Elliott

Pinyon Publishing
MONTROSE, CO

Cover Painting by Susan E. Elliott

Photographs by Susan E. Elliott & Gary L. Entsminger

Book and Cover Design by Susan E. Elliott

First Edition: April 2013

Pinyon Publishing
23847 V66 Trail, Montrose, CO 81403
www.pinyon-publishing.com

Library of Congress Control Number: 2013904504
ISBN: 978-1-936671-13-7

FOR JEAN ZIPP

Contents

It is a willow when summer is over,
a willow by the river
from which no leaf has fallen nor
bitten by the sun
turned orange or crimson.
The leaves cling and grow paler,
swing and grow paler
over the swirling waters of the river
as if loath to let go,
they are so cool, so drunk with
the swirl of the wind and of the river—
oblivious to winter,
the last to let go and fall
into the water and on the ground.

—William Carlos Williams

In sleep she knew she was in her bed, but not the bed she had lain down in a few hours since, and the room was not the same but it was a room she had known somewhere.

—Katherine Anne Porter

Once a youthful pair,
Fill'd with softest care,
Met in garden bright
Where the holy light
Had just remov'd the curtains of the night.

There, in rising day,
On the grass they play;
Parents were afar,
Strangers came not near,
And the maiden soon forgot her fear.

—William Blake

We cannot kindle when we will
The fire which in the heart resides;
The spirit bloweth and is still,
In mystery our soul abides.

—Matthew Arnold

No, I will rob Tellus of her weed,
To strew thy green with flowers. The yellows, blues,
The purple violets, and marigolds,
Shall, as a carpet, hang upon thy grave
While summer days doth last. Ay me, poor maid,
Born in a tempest when my mother died,
This world to me is a lasting storm,
Whirring me from my friends.

—Marina in *Pericles* by William Shakespeare

Turtle

I wake not knowing where I am. Someone taps a washboard. *Click, clacking*. Nathaniel's wife, Naomi. I see her on their porch back home in our valley between Buena Vista and Lexington near the South River beneath the Blue Ridge Mountains.

I rub my eyes, and the dream goes back where dreams arise. I hear a *train tracking*. I lift the velvet curtain and look out. It's dark as a blister. The whistle of another train gets louder and higher as it flashes by in an instant. In the light of one car a girl's head is bent forward reading.

When did I fall asleep? It had been dark along the New River in West Virginia. But this time of year it gets dark early wherever you are in the northern hemisphere. That's a fact. The earth tilts. Doc says. He knows astronomy. He's my father, a doctor, and that's why we're going to Colorado.

We must have crossed the Ohio River overnight. Darn, I wanted to see it. From now on I'll stay awake, even when I'm sleeping. I love hearing Uncle Charles and Nathaniel play that rolling one, "Big Sandy River." When Nathaniel picks the banjo, it's like no one else, while Charles runs the bass notes and strums the chords on his guitar. Sings too when he has a mind to. And sometimes they go into the parlor where Mama accompanies them on piano.

—What's that one? I asked.

—"Big Sandy," Charles said. Named for the Ohio.

—How's that?

Doc chimed in:

—In the old days some places had more than one name. The Ohio River was also the Big Sandy because it had so many sand bars.

—You like that one, Miss Eva? Nathaniel asked.

—Yes. Very much.

They played it again for me.

My grandfather Poppy said:

—When you awake, I won't be there.

—But you said you'd always be with me.

—Yes, and I will be.

I was on my way to get eggs for Rosa when Poppy stopped me, propping his foot on an elm stump.

—What did you dream?

I rubbed my eye with one fist.

—How much do you want to know?

—As much as you want to tell me. Or write it down, soon as you're awake enough to find a pencil.

—Why's that?

—So you won't forget.

—Why's that?

—It's our nature; we forget. For some it's easier that way. We have to want to remember, Eva, my darling.

So as soon as I'm awake I switch on the light and write.

Last night I was with Aunt Katie in her glider swinging in the sunshine beside her flower beds. She said:

—The glider needs painting.

She wore her long apron. Peonies were blooming. Poppies nodded scarlet heads. I saw the pond past the mill. The breeze blew warm. We faced the road, but no one came by.

Wait a minute. The pond wasn't where it should have been. That's the way with dreams; they fool you if the details aren't right. And you don't know if you're dreaming or if it's day or night. But Aunt Katie was fretting about June bugs, so I know for sure I was dreaming.

2

TURTLE

She waved her arm to send a bug flying, and then suddenly they were everywhere, buzzing us. Then as if they weren't, she said she remembered what she wanted to tell me. Which is more evidence I'd been dreaming; she hardly remembers anything anymore because of her Alzheimer's.

Doc said:
— You need images to remember. But Aunt Katie believes they're sinful. That's what they taught in her church. She walked the mile and a half holding her mother's hand always in time for Sunday School.
— You're making that up about the images.
— Nope. Idolatry. Old Testament. God said there were to be no images of him. Or any of the other gods.
— Why?
— He knew their power.
— But isn't power a good thing?
— Can be. But some folks like Aunt Katie have always worried they'd imagine the wrong things.
— Sinful things?
— Something like that.
— But how do you think without images?
— If you think Aristotle got it right, you don't. Images *are* thinking in his book.
— Then what's the point of not having them?
— That depends on how you think and how free you want other thinkers to be.

I considered that. A couple of weeks ago my teacher Miss Powers shouted at Lewis:
— Your mind is in the gutter.
And the entire class came to a halt because we thought we knew what she meant, that he was thinking what he shouldn't, and we also knew he was embarrassed. But we didn't know what he was thinking, just that his face turned as red as one of Rosa's beets. I see her in a red and white checked apron waving goodbye from the road. That was yesterday morning. And now we're miles from there. Maybe nowhere. If you don't know where you are.

3

Grandma Rosa said:

— In fall, the veil between the earth and the spirits is thinner. The ones on the other side are closer but not necessarily more reliable. So be careful when you call to them.

I'm almost certain Lewis wasn't calling spirits, at least not intentionally, but you can bet your life you better not argue when you're in that situation. Miss Powers is an old maid, although Mama says not to call her that.

We went inside Aunt Katie's house, and I saw the painting of Jesus on her wall and said:

— Is it true that you don't see pictures in your mind?

Or something like that, I couldn't come right out and say *images* since I didn't know how she'd react. Or *in your heart*, which is another way to think about where the images are. Poppy says you should treat people kindly in your dreams, just as you would when you're not dreaming.

Her eyes wide and beaming, Aunt Katie said:

— Lord, child. What's the matter with you? The devil's got your tongue.

She reached toward my mouth, as my hand rushed to cover my lips. I couldn't have said anything even if I'd tried to.

— I'll wash your mouth out with soap. You know I will.

Then she looked away as if she'd forgotten I was there. And commenced singing:

— Come by here, my Lord, come by here.

She isn't here and I'm awake. The sun also rises. The Virginia mountains are behind us in the darkness. We're on our way to Chicago, Illinois; Santa Fe, New Mexico; and Django, Colorado. This is a train and I'm a passenger. These are the facts. But am I dreaming?

— Sometimes dreams track forward in time, Poppy said.

— How?

— Imagine a traveler. Someone you know and suppose she, your friend, is a dreamer coming from the past to your time.

—How? Why?

—She's looking for something. Perhaps the people in her village have a problem, and they need you.

—Like an attack from an enemy?

—Or a disease or drought. Who knows. But she arrives in one of your dreams.

—Is that possible?

—Of course. Anything is possible. It just might not seem logical.

—And we help her?

—If we can.

I close my notebook and look into the aisle. Doc is tucking in his shirt. He holds a finger to his lips and motions toward Mama breathing softly behind him. He pulls her curtain closed, points toward the door at the end of our compartment, and whispers:

—Breakfast.

I dress as quietly as a dormouse.

We walk toward the dining car, moving toward the back of the train, toward Virginia. I say:

—If you could walk fast enough, and if you had enough train, you could reach the farm.

Doc says:

—But you'd get awfully hungry. It would take a long time to get there at this rate.

Then I say:

—Musketeers, moon, marmalade, muchness.

Doc says:

—Monkeys, man, mushrooms, mononucleosis.

Doc's good at the Name Game. So's Billy, but he isn't here right now. And I don't expect he'll ever come to Colorado.

The dining car is a sight to see; let me tell you. Tables on each side decked out in white linen and what looks like genuine china, which has to come all the way from China. Otherwise, it's something else. Above the clattering of the kitchen and the smell of bacon, a radio broadcasts a quick tempo piano piece. As we sit, I ask:

—What kind of music is that?

—Ragtime. Scott Joplin. "Maple Leaf Rag." You like it?

—I do.

A black man in a suit with a towel draped over his arm comes toward us, and Doc says:

—Excuse me, sir. Are we too early for breakfast?

The man says:

—Yes suh, just a little. Cooks aren't ready. But I can get you a pot of coffee, and it's mighty good.

—Thanks, Doc says and then turns to me. It's about time you had your first cup of coffee. You agree?

I am astonished and sit up as straight as I can.

—What will Mama say?

—Nothing if you don't tell her. And if you do she'll say: Well, Eva May, who do you think you are? Just because you're riding a train to Colorado. And she'll put her hands on her hips like she does. Later she'll have a little something to say to me. But I'm willing to take my chances if you are.

I give him a short nod and glance around the room, trying to take it all in.

—Make that two cups, Doc says to the waiter who stands even straighter.

I look up at him and smile. He's quite tall and a little hefty.

Doc adds:

—With lots of cream.

Then I ask:

—Is it true this china came all the way from China?

He winks and says:

—Missy, you can depend on that for sure and certain.

From the observation car you can see to China almost. I touch my finger to my mouth. The bitter taste lingers although I brushed my teeth. I guess you get used to it. If I look from the right angle, I can see my reflection in the window.

> my face in
> the glass fields
> streaming past

—That's poetry, Billy'd say. A haiku. But one without enough syllables, technically.

He's going to be a poet someday. Already is. Even if he is a year older than I am, I'm an inch taller, and he knows it. Poppy's taller than both of us and straight-backed like the tulip poplar by the pond. He taught me *learning by heart* before I started school. And I taught Billy this fall. He's my friend, my boyfriend you might say, although some would say I'm too young for that.

—Look around the room, I said to Billy. See Doc's desk. That's his inkwell and pen. (*I pointed.*) Now close your eyes. Take a deep breath, and don't breathe again for five seconds. Count. (*I took a deep breath too.*) Imagine you're light as a feather. Do you see Doc's desk? Do you see a stack of books? Is Doc sitting there? With your eyes closed. Tell me.

—It's blurry.

—Then open your eyes and look again, closely this time. It's as easy as falling off a log, Grandma Rosa says. God takes care of the rest.

—God? She sees God?

—Not exactly … Well, I don't know.

—Then how does she know he takes care of it?

I thought about that.

—Billy Morgan, just because you're from California doesn't mean you know everything. She just knows. I just know. And even if I don't know, which is something you wouldn't know, if you pay attention, you might learn something.

That got him. Billy does not like to be told there's something he doesn't know. So he closed his eyes and in no time at all had the hang of it.

Mama walks into the observation car and sits beside me. I try not to be nervous as I wait for the question. I imagine somewhere I like to be: my lookout, the big group of rocks—calcite, Doc says—that look out over the farm, just up the slope across the road. From there you can see it all: the fields, the pond, Aunt Katie's, the garden, and sometimes Nathaniel and Uncle Charles at the mill.

But Mama looks out the window and says:

—Silos for corn. We must be getting close to Indianapolis.

—It's been an hour since sunrise.

—Did you enjoy your … oatmeal?

—Yes ma'am.

When the train slows, the conductor bellows as if we're all hard of hearing:

—Union Station. Union Station.

Red brick buildings. Doc comes into the observation car.

—Do you two want to get out and stretch your legs? This is the oldest Union Station in the world. God knows when we'll be here again.

—There's more than one? I ask.

—Almost always. We're a country of people who like to repeat ourselves.

We step down to the platform and walk into an enormous room.

You wouldn't believe it, Ave. I'm sure glad I found you. I miss you.

Ave's taller than I am and thin as a sapling. I imagine her looking up at the ceiling arching over us. She points to a large circular window at one end of the great room. Twenty feet in diameter I'd say, using my hands and eyes to measure the way Doc taught me. Look closer and you can see that the window consists of five concentric circles, divided by rays like the spokes of a bicycle wheel. And between each ray small rectangular sections sparkle with colored glass.

Can you see that? I write to Billy. It's my first letter to anyone. Billy gave me stationery when he said goodbye: a notepad and a little red box of envelopes. I bought the stamps with my allowance. Three cents apiece, Admiral Byrd Expedition II, and the world map on the stamp is like the window in Union Station.

And is that a coincidence? Poppy would ask.

I see him back on the farm, hundreds of miles from here, walking toward the horses. Sargent, the white, stands tall and lifts one big hoof to paw the earth. Poppy lets me ride him, although he's not really a riding horse.

I think about that as we walk around the crowded Union Station which is noisy with voices, shuffling feet, and a loud speaker announcing one thing after another. Doc sets a coin on a plate a man holds up to him. I ask Mama if that's someone Doc knows. She doesn't answer. We pass several more men like that, but Doc only nods to the others and says:

—I'm sorry.

Later he says to Mama:

—Leah, it's worse than I thought.

The men are polite and dressed well enough. One's in a brown sports jacket, but they don't look at me or Mama.

We get back on the train and return to our sleeping compartment, which has been turned back into a regular train car with seats facing each other. Doc says:

—A marvel of technology.

He opens his book. Mama pulls out her knitting. I open my notebook. Poppy says a notebook is important for jogging your memory. So I write. If I work hard, I can become a writer some day, Doc says, or a scientist.

Twenty days ago, October 18, 1933, Wednesday, Turtle. The bus let Billy and me off at Honey Hollow, which winds up the hill to our farm. As usual, we were the only two who got off there. Mr. Macky's bus, a Blue Bird number 21, is usually empty by the time we reach our stop. Only Jenny Lynn Lauck and her three brothers live farther up the main road, and they don't come to school regularly. Mostly they keep to themselves. We watched Mr. Macky turn the bus around, and then we started walking.

It's a mile up to our farm past our neighbors, which you can count on two hands: Clarks, Floyds, Fitzgeralds (they're Irish), Williams, Hayslettes, Clarks again, Stuarts, Billy's house, Aunt Katie's, and us. Uncle Charles' and Nathaniel and Naomi's cabins are up in the woods above the farm and hidden from the road.

Billy and I walked beside the creek. The sycamores were smooth, shiny white-barked, and their leaves had begun to fall. The blackbirds were gathering, cackling, talking to each other, one branch to another. We stopped where the creek pools and tossed in leaves, watching them swirl downstream. I asked Billy if he wanted to play Invisible Universe.

—What's that?

—A game. One of us names a person, place, or thing and describes it. The other has to guess if it's in the Visible or Invisible Universe.

—What do you mean *Invisible Universe*?

—Whether I'm imagining it. If it's in the *Invisible* Universe, I'm imagining it. If it's something anyone can see, it's in the *Visible* Universe.

—How will I know if you're telling the truth?

—That's the first rule. You have to tell the truth. Otherwise, there's no point in playing.

—Then what?

—We switch, and the other person describes something. It's easy. We'll learn from each other.

—How's that?

—Anything you tell me that's in the Visible Universe that I don't already know about will be new for me, and I can add it to my Visible Universe.

—And if it's in the Invisible Universe?

—Even better. I learn something you're imagining. Poppy and I play when we're working in the garden. He says it's especially appropriate there because most of what happens in a garden happens in the Invisible Universe.

—How's that?

—You ever see a tomato turn red? In front of your eyes, I mean.

—Well, not exactly.

—That's because tomatoes turn red in the Invisible Universe.

—But I see them after they turn red.

—Of course you do; then they're in the Visible Universe.

—So things can go from one universe to the other.

—Yes. That's what's so interesting, don't you think?

Billy moved here just before school started in August. One evening he and his dad came over to our farm and introduced themselves. Mr. Morgan's a talker like Doc. But Billy didn't say much that time. Mostly he sat listening to the men. Since Doc and Mr. Morgan like to talk about books, they hit it off from the start. Billy barely noticed me, or didn't seem to. Then Rosa asked me to help in the kitchen. When we were done, Billy and his dad were gone. Billy's a year older than I am, but we only have four rooms in our school, so sixth and seventh grades share a room. That's where he started noticing me, and we got to know each other walking home.

We said goodbye at the bridge that runs over Mill Creek, and I ran up to the garden beside the house where Mama and Poppy were picking tomatoes.

—Afternoon, Eva, Poppy said without looking up.

I set my books down, tucked my dress up around my legs, and began picking. The sun felt like the Lord's own hand: bright, warm, and stretching across the land. I was glad my dress was light.

—Ah, cotton, I said. I love it. It makes me want to dance. Where does it come from?

—From down in the land of cotton, Mama said. Alabama.

—That's a long way to haul it.

—They haul it even farther than that. To the North on boats, where they make it into fabric and send it back to us so I can sew your dresses.

—That doesn't make sense at all.

—It does if you don't know how to make fabric or can't grow cotton. Which starts dull creamy-white. Dirty by some standards. Someone has to dye it so you'll want to wear it.

—Can't we dye it here?

She looked at Poppy, then said to me:

—Now that you're here to help, I'll go in and practice. Hand me your books. And don't bruise my Brandywines. We've been waiting long enough for them to ripen.

—Yes, ma'am, I won't.

We heard the piano, slow and melancholy. I didn't recognize the song, but sometimes Mama composes her own pieces, mixing bits from tunes she learned growing up in Austria. Poppy says you can hear her ancestry in her music more than in her speech. I guess it's because she started learning English when she was seven. She speaks pretty much like the rest of us but not on the piano. I've never heard anyone play like her. She taught me Bartók's *Melodies For Children*.

> I lost my young couple
> Dawn, O day
> Clutching her handkerchief

Bartók's Hungarian. I want to play like Mama when I grow up.

After our dry summer the tomato vines were crinkled along their edges. A monarch butterfly gliding beside the garden turned to light on a vine near Poppy's shoulder. He already had a full basket of tomatoes. I said:

—Doc says the monarch butterflies fly all the way to Mexico for winter.

—Is that right?

—Yes, sir.

—They better get a move on. Your grandma thinks it's going to frost.

—So are we picking all the green ones?

—Only the shiny ones that have a touch a' yellow. The others can wait. I'm not going to disagree with Rosa, but between you and me, I think it's a few degrees too early yet to frost. And this crop has had a hard enough growing season. Might as well give it a few more nights after this long. It's a good thing we all like fried green tomatoes.

—With onions, I said, squatting at the far end of the row.

The rows are short, and we were in easy talking distance. Poppy said:

—What did you do at school today?

—Oh you know, the usual, and we got our history essays back.

—What did you write about?

—The Civil War.

—Ah. And what did you say?

—Over six hundred thousand people died in it.

—That's a lot of people. Why were so many people killing each other?

—It's a little confusing, but I think it was because the South had slaves.

—And the North didn't?

—I don't think so. Up there, people worked in factories instead of on farms.

—Ah, I guess they didn't need slaves for that.

—I guess not. But we don't need slaves to farm here.

—That's right, Eva, and our family didn't have slaves during the Civil War either.

We were quiet, picking, covered in the smell of vine thickness. When we met in the middle of the row my basket was half full.

When I turned to show Poppy he was already looking at me.

Poppy knew it was time to tell her. Doc and Leah had decided it would be easier on Eva coming from him. Grandfathers have special status with granddaughters.

Doc had come home that afternoon with the letter saying they welcomed him to start a practice in Django, Colorado. Poppy's friend, Esperanza Domingo-Rodriguez, had set everything in motion. But the family had known a change had been coming for a decade since Doc had returned late from the War in 1920. Leah was with him, and Eva was not far behind. He came home expecting relief from what he had experienced in Europe, but he found a different kind of war here. The American newspapers said it was the Germans who experimented on their own people. And that is possible; people do unspeakable things. But he hadn't expected the people in his own town to be unspeakable.

Like Poppy's mother Iris said:

— You don't need the right moral arguments if you know the right words to get what you want.

Doc had stood by his morals, and now it was catching up with him and his family.

Eva picked up her basket and stood. A small falcon, a kestrel, flew above the vines. Its shadow skimmed Poppy's face looking up at her. And with an even sweep of wings, the bird halted in the air as if considering a mystery. Seconds later, it fluttered and sailed like an arrow over the pond.

Eva said before he had a chance:

— Who taught you to garden?

— Lots of folks. My mother and father. Neighbors, friends. We all learned from each other.

— What kinds of things?

— Where to plant. Which plants grow better with others. How to feed the soil. Our ancestors knew a lot about growing food. They had to. They provided for themselves. They had to know which plants were nutritious and how to preserve what they harvested.

— And they passed that on to us.

— That's right.

— We had some smart ancestors.

— That's right. And we wouldn't be here today if they hadn't

been so smart.
—That makes sense.

Then Poppy said:
—Some news came today.
She waited, trying to read his eyes.
—What kind of news?

I could see it. His eyes looked tired and worried at the same time, big brown like simmering apple butter. He tucked his long loose hair behind his ears. Something was wrong.

Then he surprised me.
—Describe someone.
—Who?
—Your grandmother.
—Where?
—In the kitchen.

I closed my eyes and took a deep breath.
—Rosa leans over the cookstove, lifts one of the stove top lids and checks the fire. Wood crackles. She moves the spider to a hotspot and sets a pan on it.
—What does she look like?
—She's tall. Her hair, brown reddish, rolled and tied. But that's not unusual. She hardly ever wears it down, and it always frizzes around her face by the end of the day, even if it is tied back. She blows it from her eyes.
—And her eyes?
—Hazel. No. Yes.

I had to think about it. It's not so easy looking into her eyes. She sees everything.
—With a twist of green, I sighed.
—Go on.
—Now she's talking to Mama. Who's come into the kitchen.

Rosa says she doesn't need help with supper, that she wants Mama to play for her instead. Then she's alone again, standing over the stove, stirring. Mama's playing. I smell tomatoes and onions. Then Rosa moves to the kitchen table and rolls out dough, her arms firm from kneading, churning butter, and digging in the garden. I run to hug her. She sees me coming and dusts off her hands on her apron.

Then I stopped. As if I had been spinning, I reached for the ground for balance. She'd been crying. I could see that now. But it was too late.

—I see them …
—Who Eva?
But I couldn't say, only:
—I know why Mama went inside.
I put down my basket and ran.

He found her at the high end of the pasture, sitting near the woods, chin cradled in her hands, looking down toward the mill. The smell of wet mud rose from the creek. An indigo bunting sang from a treetop as he stepped toward her, and hearing him she stood and slipped into his arms. Time paused as they rocked in one motion. Then he unfolded his arms and urged her toward the house, the sun disappearing into a westerly breeze and the wheel turning.

—Do you hear that? Poppy asked.
—Yes, Nathaniel and Charles went back to work. I saw them when I came up here.
—Ah, yes. And you were a few minutes later coming home today.
Eva stopped, a few steps from the grape arbor that goes up to the pantry and kitchen. Poppy said:
—Billy's a good boy.
—But I'll never see him again.

—Of course you will. You'll see him every day you want to.

—But no new memories, she said, her eyes declaring awareness.

—That's not entirely true.

—Visits, I know. But realistically, Poppy, we'll be two thousand miles away from each other!

—Realistically, Eva. If you can travel that far, so can he.

—When are we leaving?

—In a few weeks.

—Why can't you come with us?

—I have to take care of the farm. Rosa needs my help.

—She can come too.

—You know she can't. She was born and raised up the holler. Her whole life has always been right here.

—So has mine. And I want to be with you.

—Then listen. I'll tell you a secret.

—A secret?

—Yes, but it's also a story, and you'll have to help me remember it.

—Do I know the story?

—Not yet.

As the train rocks, my notebook slides right and left on my lap. Doc says:

—Here, use this. It's a lap desk, a writing surface tacked to a pillow. Clever, no? It'll make it easier to write.

He sets it on my lap, and I close my eyes as if for dreaming. I remember how Poppy's story starts.

Long ago before we wrote things down, we related stories by firelight and moonlight, during ceremonies and to help pass the long hours. We knew we must remember where we had been and who we were.

Our people came from Turtle Island, which was off the coast of North America. People of many tribes came from nearby islands to trade and commune with our people. Sometimes a Turtle man married a visiting woman, and the new couple left to live with her people. These comings and goings went on as long as anyone could remember.

One tribe came from an island much farther east. They had skin and hair as white and lucid as the moon. They were clever, and the Turtle Island people welcomed their new ideas. After the ceremonies, a few of the East Island women did not return with their people but instead stayed on Turtle Island to marry Turtle men, and their children became a new Turtle people, our ancestors.

The Turtle Islanders lived peacefully and prospered until the great flood when our island was drowned and survivors escaped on boats, rowing west to higher shores.

Many years passed. Then one day, a towering ship brought another tribe of people from the east. The newcomers were also fair-skinned but not as milky white as the people who had come to Turtle Island long before. Our Turtle Island people, who were now part of the Shore people, called the newcomers *the golden ones* because their skin was like the autumn grasses that make the golden hills. The golden ones, in turn, acknowledged their specialness by keeping to themselves and building strange houses at the mouth of the Sacred River. At first, the Shore people pitied the newcomers who did not take to the land well and became sick in winter. Also, there were no women among them, which was very strange.

Then something happened that changed everything.

Whirlwind

Leaves whirl past the window. The train whistles at a crossing. A boy standing beside a Model A Ford near the tracks waves as we pass. He looks about the same age as Billy, and our farm flashes in my mind, as we drove away in Poppy's Model A.

I see Billy the day after I knew we were leaving.

We were walking home from the bus stop. A hermit thrush whistled from the woods, its hollow notes ethereal and flute-like. The long shadows disappeared into deeper darkness. Indian summer, but the speckled red and yellow leaves swirling past our feet reminded us that winter was coming. Seeing us, a squirrel gathering acorns scurried up a chestnut oak. Billy was jabbering about a man who boats up a river in the Congo in a novel he'd been reading.

— Looking for someone or lost? I asked.

— Both.

We passed Aunt Katie's. I don't think Billy noticed the thrush.

But it's hard to know what anyone notices if they don't let you in on it. And Billy's harder than most. He's not from here; he grew up in San Francisco in an apartment above a busy street. He said you could hear sirens in the dead of night.

— That doesn't sound like a good place to live.

— Not everything was bad. You could always smell good Chinese food cooking. And the Chinese people are friendly.

Whistling interrupts my train of thought. I look up, then return to writing. I have to concentrate harder now to see Billy. And he's not where I left him. He's by the window in our classroom and turns to look at me while Miss Powers writes on the blackboard.

Her chalk screeched as she recited:

— It is I; it is he; it is she; it is we; it is they; you, who, it. Say it again. I can't hear you.

We all know she can tell who's reciting and who's not without turning around. When she did turn, her glasses were low on her nose, and she held the chalk in front of her puffy white blouse. Her black skirt barely covered her knees. She's a big woman, but I wouldn't call her fat.

Then I see Billy walking beside me again, and past him Uncle Charles' cabin edges the woods and pasture. If you know where it is you can see it behind the leaves. Charles talks to birds, but he'd claim he didn't if you asked him. He's tall and handsome like Doc and lives alone. I once heard Mrs. Stuart (she's the fourth and fifth grade teacher) call him a ladies' man. But you'd think if he were, I'd have an aunt by now. They say I almost had one. But no matter how hard I try I can't picture her.

When we got to the bridge by the mill, Billy said:

— What's bothering you?

— What?

— You've been staring into space the whole way home. You didn't even ask me the title of the book.

— I have? I didn't?

He looked puzzled. I said:

— I'm sorry.

He stopped, leaned against the railing on the bridge, and looked into the shallow creek.

— It's OK. I just thought something might be wrong.

— I'm fine (*not wanting to tell him yet*), but thanks.

I stood on the bridge watching him walk back down the lane. Books in his left arm, right hand in his jacket pocket. As he passed Aunt Katie's he looked toward the woods.

The mill wheel turned like a ferris wheel at a carnival. If you were small enough, you could ride the wheel up and over and back down. I wonder if they have carnivals in Colorado. Doc said they have rodeos.

As I neared the house, Kleela came running and jumped up, her paws on my stomach. I scratched her black head. She isn't supposed to jump up, so I pushed her down and kneeled to hug her.

—Did you miss me?

We passed the garden, where most of the vines were dry and empty except for a few tomatoes Poppy and I had left to ripen. Then we hurried up the steps and across the porch to the kitchen doorway where Rosa was waiting. I hugged her. Then she nudged me inside where Mama was counting jars of freshly made tomato and onion relish. I set my books on a chair, and Mama turned and kissed me, running her fingers through my hair. Then Rosa handed me a jar and a covered basket.

—Take this up to Naomi and hurry back.

—Sure, what's in it? Smells like biscuits.

—Yes, and tell her this is the only jar that didn't seal, so they need to eat it soon. Nathaniel can pick up the rest of their jars later.

—When's our supper?

She handed me a biscuit and said:

—This will hold you over. Now hurry back, and don't wander in the woods.

Then she said:

—This time of year the veil between the worlds is thinner. You know what that means, don't you?

—Yes, ma'am. The spirits on the other side are closer to us.

—But not necessarily more reliable.

—Yes, ma'am.

—And you can cross over without knowing it. So pay attention to where you are.

—Yes, ma'am.

Eva and Kleela walked up the creek together. The goldenrods were finishing their blooms on one side, and the grasses were tall and tan. Where the race splits off, Eva's eyes followed the diversion down to the mill wheel. Charles and Nathaniel were on the porch smoking pipes. Nathaniel lowered a tender gaze on his banjo, which leaned against the railing, catching rays of sunlight.

What was probably the last wagon of the day had just rolled away, and you could hear the driver yelling to his horses, rising from the hard seat, urging the reins as the loaded wagon started down the lane toward town.

Charles and Nathaniel watched the wheel turn as if something important were about to happen. Each trough poured water into the tailrace before it disappeared beneath the wheel. When they saw Eva, she held up the basket and waved. Kleela splashed on ahead of her. Eva hummed one of the *Melodies For Children* as she crossed the creek and climbed the hill to the cabin in the woods.

> Let's bake something
> It should be round
>
> Let's play something
> Full of sound
>
> Let's find something
> Not easily found.

Naomi wasn't there, so I wrote a note about the seal and left it with the basket inside. I could have skipped the note because she'd see for herself, but I knew Rosa would ask.

There was still sunlight, so I decided to explore, just a little, before going home. I crossed back over the creek and followed it down: splitting at the diversion, where it goes either over to the wheel or into the pond and then under the road and south toward town. I left it and crossed the field at the base of Irish Mountain, a launching point for the grand spine of mountains that we call the Blue Ridge. I didn't intend to go far, just up to the ridge for a good lookout. The mountain goes a long way from there, but I've never been that far.

I followed the deer trail. Mama's rule is to stay in sight, so I looked down on the mill where Nathaniel was adjusting his banjo strap. A little farther I saw a snippet of the South river. I imagined a feather starting in the creek below and floating from one river into the next: the South, the Maury, the James, all the way to the Atlantic ocean.

At the ridge, I heard a thrush sing from the Invisible Universe. I kneeled in the crunchy leaves beside the trail and squinted into the sliver of light between us. Squinting can help you see more than you usually do. As I tried to make out the thrush I remembered the first time I saw Ave.

A starry night. I was in bed when Poppy came to the door and said:
— If you stay absolutely still, you can hear her.
Then he pulled my door almost closed and left. I took the quilt from my bed, wrapped it around me, and sat on the chair beside the window. The wind was whistling, but I kept the window open and listened. A barn owl hooted. I closed my eyes, but I didn't intend to fall asleep. I focused on the tea party I had been reading about earlier. Three places had been set (for Hare, Hatter, and Dormouse) when Alice appeared unexpectedly.
And Hare said:
— Take some more tea.
Alice replied in an offended tone:
— I've had nothing yet, so I can't take more.
Then Hatter said:
— You mean you can't take less; it's easy to take more than nothing.

I had been wondering how more or less worked when I must have fallen asleep. I was dreaming, walking along the creek on a warm spring morning. The sun streamed between sycamores creating a pattern, like a tablecloth beneath the canopy. I smelled violets and honeysuckle. Someone was singing. Two short notes rose, and one long note dove into a deeper place. I thought I heard my name, and someone said:

—Open your eyes.

A girl jumped from a branch, auburn hair shimmering, then disappeared, and reappeared, or I thought she did, but it was a bird this time.

Then a girl was there looking at me.

Then I was back in the darkness of my room, the rest of the dream lost, except the girl, and I didn't even know her name.

Names are important; they help us remember who and what things are. A *bird*, she was a bird; I just knew it. I lit a candle and crept downstairs to Doc's study and found a book of Zoology. Birds are in a Class called *Aves*, I read. Aves. That made me think of Mama's record, "Ave Maria," by Schubert. Mama used to play it for me when I was little, to help me fall asleep. *Aves, Ave, Eva*. That's it. Good night, my Ave. *Gute Nacht*.

I opened my eyes. The thrush had stopped singing. Kleela was watching a squirrel watching her. The sun was starting to set. Shadows covered the trail, and I knew it was time to hurry home.

Billy and Eva sat at the kitchen table working on a history assignment. Doc and Leah had gone into the study shortly after supper, and Rosa was in the large open room working on a quilt. Poppy went out to the porch and lit his pipe. As he looked across to Irish Mountain, Billy and Eva came outside to join him. Eva sat on the swing beside Poppy. Her legs crossed at the ankles, she rested her head against his shoulder. Poppy pushed the swing slowly back and forth with one foot. Billy leaned against a post nearby, one leg dangling off the edge. Sometimes he looked toward the fields that sloped from the house. But mostly he watched Eva when he thought she wasn't noticing. He sensed something had changed, but he couldn't put his finger on it.

Poppy said:

— Would like you to hear more of the story?

— Yes, they said.

A small group of the golden ones were canoeing up the Chickahominy River, which is named for the people who crush corn. Some believe the Chickahominy descended from the moon people, who came here long ago with their new methods of farming. We still call their special corn *rockahominy* or *hominy*.

The golden ones were looking for gold not corn.

From tall longleaf pines a small hunting band watched the golden chief and three companions pole past in a canoe. The golden chief seemed to look upriver. But he knew he was being watched, not only by the Chickahominy hunting band but also by the Powhatan, who were displeased to see intruders. The golden chief, outnumbered and not intending to fight, let himself be captured.

The Powhatan tribe was known for their feathered headbands, which harnessed the spirits of great eagles. They were powerful dreamers, descendents of ancient Iroquois that once roamed the eastern woodlands from Canada to Virginia. They believed that nothing happens until it's dreamed.

Their chief, Wahunsenacawh (which means *principal dreamer*), sent word to the priests and elders of the Chickahominy that he wanted their young seer to attend the trial of the golden chief, who had been captured on the Chickahominy River, which meant that the Chickahominy people, by tribal law, had some say in what was to become of the golden chief.

The Chickahominy did not allow chiefs to rule them. Instead, all tribal decisions were carried out by a group of priests and elders called *cawcawassaughes*. Their young seer, Chickacawcaw, whom Wahun had summoned, was called *Chick* for short. He was a brave young man who had been trained as a priest. He had many clear visions. The tribe valued his abilities to see into the future and to communicate with other tribes.

The tribal council convened in Wahun's longhouse, along the low shore of the Sacred River, where a gray haze rested and then ran to the sea in vanishing flatness. Chick attended and watched. He knew his being asked to participate was merely custom and not because Wahun valued his opinion. Wahun's younger half-brother, Opechancanough, was a great warrior, and he and his men had, after all, captured the golden chief. Opechancanough means *he whose soul is white*. Opech's mother came from a race of white-skinned mountain people who were even more powerful dreamers. Some said she had been banished from the mountains and passed her anger into her son, who was always ready for a fight.

Opech brought the golden chief before his older brother Wahun in the longhouse and argued that the golden chief should be slain immediately:

— These golden ones do not know how to communicate with the spirits of birds or trees. They are unfit to live on the back of the great Turtle. They are ignorant, like children, yet they think they understand the creator.

Wahun considered this and was about to agree when his daughter Matoaka, who had been standing silently at the edge of the council, hurried forward, and knelt before him.

— Spare the golden chief, and I will teach him how to know the spirits of our land so his people too can live in harmony.

Matoaka was Wahun's favorite, which allowed her to get away with rule-breaking that would have gotten anyone else in big trouble. She was twelve years old, bright and spirited, but seemed older. Chick was moved by her courage.

—How will you do this? her father asked.

—I will dream a way, she said softly. I have seen these golden ones in my dreams.

This made several men in the council laugh. But Matoaka's eyes stayed her father's judgement. Wahun loved and respected his daughter, and he knew she had unusual gifts.

—I will let you try, my daughter.

There were murmurings among the council, but no one dared oppose the chief. Chick silently agreed with Matoaka. But Opech was not appeased. His eyes fired with enmity. Since he could not confront Wahun, he glared instead at Chick. His anger sought the princess too, but she avoided his eyes.

Wahun said to Chick:

—Since the violation occurred along your tribe's part of the river, you will be responsible for guarding the golden chief. My warriors will accompany you back to your village. My daughter Matoaka will go there each morning until the new moon. If by then the golden chief has learned the ways of the spirits, we will return him to his people.

Of course Wahun didn't trust the golden chief, and he sent several of his most trusted warriors to guard the princess each time she went to Chick's village.

Although the princess didn't tell Chick what she saw in her dreams, he could see her magic working as she taught the golden chief about plants, herbs, and the words he must use when he called the spirits. Still the golden chief learned slowly, and the princess would have needed to defend him again had Wahun not lost interest. At the beginning of the next moon cycle, a band of Chick's warriors rowed the golden chief downriver and left him near his village.

The golden chief had been captured in late fall. The following spring his people tried to implement the new farming methods, but they were more interested in tobacco than corn. Chick watched them from the woods. Smoking tobacco was a sacred activity, and he thought the golden ones could benefit from his help. He sent a messenger to ask the golden chief to come to Chick's village for instruction. But the golden chief sent another man, who was inquisitive and returned to Chick's village several times. Chick's people called him Talutah because his face got so red when he smoked tobacco. The princess and Talutah became good friends.

Hearth

Although not as crowded as it would be the following day for the continuous cooking and stirring of apples into butter, the house buzzed with family and neighbors who came to help prepare the apples in a festive display of washing, coring, peeling, chopping, laughter, and small talk.

Billy wasn't sure he'd heard right when Floyd asked Doc if the family had found a place to live in Colorado. He'd been coring apples with Nathaniel's oldest daughter Rachael and now looked over to Eva, who was peeling with her head down. The women beside her at the table barely took breaths in their conversation, but Eva wasn't listening. When she could no longer resist the pressure, she looked up and met Billy's eyes.

Doc said:

— A little house on the edge of town. It has a second building used before as an apartment that I can remodel for my practice.

— That right? Katie said, despite being not much interested in anything that goes on beyond the county, even if Doc was family. (*She nodded to her apple, a long spiral peel curving away from her knife.*) I'll be a monkey's uncle.

The details and casual certainty increased the blow to Billy. The next time Eva got up to go to the cold cellar for more apples, he slipped outside behind her.

I had planned to get the next batch of apples when the bin was low. But Charles had to tease me before I got a chance.

— Miss Eva May, we've caught up with you. Am I going to have to take over your job?

— Will you listen to him? Aunt Katie cooed, looking up at the other ladies peeling. The manager apparently has too much talk and not enough work of his own.

— What's that? Charles said and gave Aunt Katie a wink that made her blush.

— Be right back, I said and took the empty crate out the back door.

Billy was right behind me, and I knew he was hurt. But I hadn't wanted to tell him until the time was right. Neither of us said anything until we got to the cellar where he blocked the door with his arm. It was dark; there was no moon. I could feel my heart in my throat.

— What's this talk of leaving?

— I ... I just found out day before yesterday.

He cocked his head, and I knew he didn't think much of my excuse since we'd walked to and from the bus stop yesterday and today.

— Colorado! That's almost as far as San Francisco.

He sounded agitated, just like a man, like Charles when he's angry. Then he stepped from the door and crossed his arms. But I knew he was more hurt than angry. I set the crate down and sat on the grassy slope, my arms locked around my knees, hoping he'd join me. He kept his distance.

I said:

— I didn't think it'd actually get worked out.

Billy was listening, but he didn't look at me. I tried to explain, but I didn't know enough, just a few things I'd heard in passing.

— Doc has been frustrated with folks in town since he came back from the War.

— Frustrated about what? You weren't even born then.

— Well, almost. But I'm not sure exactly. I've overheard him

30

talking with Mama, and he says some things aren't as they used to be. I think something is wrong, maybe with his practice. He gives away most of his work. Maybe people owe him money.

—But why does that mean he has to leave and take you with him? It can't be that bad. He's lived here all his life. Everybody likes him. That's obvious.

—I don't think everybody. Well, I'm not sure. I wish I were. All I know is this started before you came. Doc started getting letters from someone in Colorado. I guess the area's growing, and they need more doctors.

I put my head in my hands and waited for Billy. After a minute that felt like ten, he sat next to me. His sleeve brushed mine.

—I don't like it, he said, looking straight ahead.

—We're not leaving for a few weeks.

He shook his head, took a long breath.

—Jiminy Crickets, he exhaled. They don't give you much time do they? They can't pull you out of school half way through the semester. Before Christmas?

—Before Thanksgiving.

Billy ran his fingers through his sandy hair, which I could see, even in the dim light, needed a trim. I think he likes it that way, covering his ears, trying to be different, like the writers he admires.

An owl hooted. I tried to smile, feeling a little better that it was out in the open. I cupped my hands around my mouth and called:

—Hoo, hoo-hoo, hoo, hoo.

The owl answered:

—Hoo, hoo-hoo, hoo, hoo.

I whispered to Billy:

—Who is it?

—Barn owl?

—No, great horned.

—Hoo-hoo hoo-hoo, Billy said.

—No, listen: Hoo, hoo-hoo, hoo, hoo.

Billy smiled.

—You sure are something.

Each of us carried a crate of apples back to the house, and when we entered, Charles called:

—Hoo, hoo-hoo, hoo, hoo.

Others laughed, and later, as the women cleaned up, the men gathered round them.

After the first tobacco harvest with the golden ones, Chick's dreams grew troubled and disrupted his sleep. One night, a fawn ran alone through a dark forest, frightened, as if being hunted. But Chick saw no hunter, and the deer disappeared. An owl screeched, and Chick felt someone beside him. But when he tried to turn his head, he couldn't; he was paralyzed. He forced himself awake, sweating and thinking about the princess, Matoaka.

Night after night he dreamed, and although the dreams differed in detail, he always woke thinking about Matoaka. Having no wife to console him, he began an exercise to calm his mind. Since the princess' image appeared to him each time he woke, he focused on her each night as he was falling asleep. He also felt that the day the golden chief was captured was important, so he reconstructed that day's events as he entered his dreams.

The day the golden chief had been captured Chick had awakened early and hiked south along the eastern bank of the Chickahominy toward where it meets the Sacred River. He swam across the wide mouth of the Chickahominy and walked to the neighboring village. He greeted his good friend, Winkapew, whose daughter was expecting a baby soon. Then Wink accompanied Chick to the corn-grinding huts. The women blushed to see the men in the early morning, but they proudly displayed the coarse-ground corn that was their speciality. They handed Wink a small pouch, which he carried to a field of new corn plants. There, he handed the pouch to Chick, who said a prayer and launched a handful of corn high into the wind. When he returned to the river, a canoe was waiting with the news that Opech had captured the golden chief.

Night after night the golden chief was captured and recaptured. When Chick woke each morning, he thought about his dreams, but he couldn't make sense of the repetition. The golden chief had been captured. But like other dreamers of his tribe, Chick expected his dreams to reveal the future. This restating of the past felt less revelatory and more organizational, what his tribe called *little dreams*.

As the summer drew on, a minor dispute between the golden ones and the Powhatans led to an attack and then a retaliation. As more attacks and retaliations ensued the Powhatans called on other tribes to join them in opposing the golden ones. They intended to expel these intruders once and for all.

The Chickahominy resisted, believing that fighting would lead to more resentment, mistrust, and vengeance. Chick had heard enough from the golden ones to believe there were plenty more of them where these had come from. He tried to remain neutral, hoping the Powhatans and golden ones would compromise and live peacefully together.

Instead of fighting, Chick and others in his tribe focused their dreams.

One night, in his mind's eye, as Chick was walking along the river, he realized the princess was walking beside him. The tall pines whispered, but neither she nor he spoke.

A few weeks later, Wahun was weakened by a mysterious illness. His medicine men could not cure him, and Wahun's desire for fighting the golden ones left him. He decided his daughter must marry, and that she and her husband would rule after he died. He knew she had been drawn to one of the golden ones, and he hoped that a marriage between them might restore peace.

But Wahun's plan did not suit Opech, who intended to become the next chief. Opech convinced Wahun that the new chief must be tested before he could rule. Since this was not uncommon among the Powhatans, Wahun agreed, expecting Opech to suggest a wrestling match or another test of physical strength. Instead Opech suggested a secret riddle. Whoever solved the riddle would marry the princess and become the new chief. But there was one caveat. If a man wagered to hear the riddle and could not solve it, his life was forfeit, and the riddle would remain a secret. Although this requirement puzzled Wahun, in his growing weakness he went along as Opech recited the riddle to each of Matoaka's fated suitors. Wahun himself could not decipher the riddle, but he trusted his brother.

> I am no viper,
> yet on a mother's babe I feed
>
> I am no farmer,
> yet I preserve the strongest seed
>
> I am no priest,
> yet sacred rose I prick to bleed
>
> In unity,
> a brother born of father
> a sister born of mother
> a husband born of mother's son
> a wife born of father's daughter
>
> What fruit does no man know to spoil
> Until first bite makes him recoil?
>
> What song when learnt through sweat and toil
> When sweetly sung will be his foil?

Most of the neighbors had left. Poppy was sitting between Eva and Billy on the porch swing. Charles and Nathaniel were standing together in the yard, discussing how early they'd arrive

34

to help with the fire the next morning. Billy, fidgeting with his hands, said to Eva:

—You remember the history assignment don't you?

—Of course, I'm done.

—What were the pages we're supposed to read?

—You know the pages: one forty to one eighty-eight.

—But which chapters?

—What?

Nathaniel was starting up the porch steps. He stopped and laughing, said to Charles:

—Yeah, I bet you will. When you're good and ready.

Charles walked off hooting. And in a hurried whisper, Billy said to Eva:

—Just get a piece of paper, will you?

So Eva ran in and got Leah's notepad from the piano bench, but before she could write the pages down, Billy said:

—Here, let me. It's you who needs it, not me.

He took the pad, scribbled something, turned it over, and handed it back, as Nathaniel said:

—You about ready to head on back to your place, Mr. Billy? I'll walk with you. I'm going that way.

—Sure, I'm all set. See ya later, Eva.

Strange, Eva thought, watching them leave.

Then she turned the pad over: *Meet me at the grape arbor when you hear me call.* Her face burned. Shivers ran down her arms and legs.

I had barely closed the door to my room when I heard him: *Hoo, hoo-hoo-hoo, hoo, hoo.* It wasn't quite right for a great horned, so I knew it was Billy. Everyone had gone to bed, but there was a light on in Doc and Mama's room. The boards creaked as I walked down the stairs and out the back door, which is the one we use when we pee outside at night. We're all accustomed to that sound—the boards creaking, I mean. Mama and Rosa use the chamber pots, but I like going outside like the men, so I can look at the stars and feel the cool night on my face. I'm not afraid of the dark.

I remember wishing it were summer, that leaving weren't so soon, that Billy had just arrived, that school had just started, and that things weren't changing so fast. Poppy says to slow down and relax, but how can anyone relax when the world is galloping away?

Billy was waiting. Behind the arbor, the lane disappeared into darkness. Sometimes I wonder what's out there in that darkness, even if I'm not afraid of it.

—We have to talk, Billy said. You can't leave.

—I don't have a choice, I whispered.

—Do you want to go?

—No ... I don't want to go.

Billy rolled his head away then back.

—We've got to figure this out. There's got to be something we can do. Here (*he spread his jacket on the ground*), the grass is wet.

We sat, our elbows almost touching as we hugged our knees. Then Billy straightened up authoritatively. I rested my chin on my knees and said:

—We just have to make these weeks count. Poppy says to remember each day so that it's crystal clear and forever in our memory.

He shook his head, said:

—This is crazy. There's no reason behind it. So your dad's a little frustrated with his job. At least he has a job. It'd be like we were switching places. I come east, and you go west. We should be in the same place.

He turned toward me. I didn't question his logic, and without knowing why, I liked the way he was acting. I looked into the darkness and tried to imagine that I wasn't leaving. But I couldn't picture it; no images rescued me.

Billy said:

—Concentrate. Unless you don't really care. Maybe you do

want to go.

My look conveyed the hurt.

—You know I don't want to go. But we can't always have our way.

He shook his head again.

—Think about it. Are you sure it's the people in town that make your dad want to leave?

—Yes, I think so. And he wants to practice more traditional medicine.

—Seems he could do that here. No offense, but that sounds like a poor reason to leave most of your family behind. Poppy and Rosa and Charles, and Nathaniel and Naomi, and your aunt. I don't think he's gonna find it's any better anywhere else. The grass is always greener. He'll probably get there and wish he'd never left home.

—Is that how you feel about San Francisco?

—That's different.

I thought about that. Maybe we'd go and find it wasn't what we imagined. Or maybe we'd get used to it. Doc keeps talking about the high snow-capped mountains like the ones Mama grew up in.

—Maybe it's Mama's idea. And maybe none of us will like it out there, and we'll turn in our tracks.

—I think there is a very high chance that you'll get there and want to turn around. There's also desert everywhere out there. Did Doc mention that?

—Even if it is desert, don't you think Doc would be embarrassed to come back? Plus, deserts aren't that bad.

—Ever been in one?

—No. But I've read about them. They have interesting animals and plants.

—Well, I've been in the Mojave Desert, and we drove across the whole state of Nevada for goodness sake. And I can tell you it's hot and dry, period.

I didn't have any response to that. So Billy said:

—Then how about this? What if he had a good reason for coming back. He could always say he'd taken a sabbatical; you

37

know, to learn some new methods. Maybe if he saw how much it hurt you to be away from the farm and Poppy ...

His eyes glinted, a flash of hope. I wanted to agree, but I said:

—I don't think doctors take sabbaticals. That's just for teachers. (*But that's when the idea hit me.*) Unless I could stay. Maybe I could stay, and they could go.

It hurt a little to say it, the idea of being away from Doc and Mama, but it might work, and then they'd want to come back to the farm because I'd still be here.

—Maybe I could convince them to let me finish the school year.

—How? There are schools in Colorado. They won't buy it.

—What if something happened?

—Like what?

—Suppose I disappeared, and we missed our train?

—How would you do that? They'd find you.

—Not if I go to my secret place in the woods.

—I don't know. You could get in a lot of trouble. And when they did find you, you'd still have to go. Only then, you'd be in real trouble.

I thought about that. It was starting to mist. I shivered. Billy said:

—We'll think of something. (*Then we stood.*) I wish I could be here tomorrow. But I have to be with Dad.

—That's OK. But maybe you can come later in the day. Come for the canning and the tasting.

—I'll try.

I wrapped my arms around myself. Now it was sprinkling.

—You're the best, Billy said.

I didn't know what to say. He stood there, and then he stepped toward me and hugged me, quickly, awkwardly I guess, but it made me shiver more. Then he was running toward the road.

—Goodbye, I said but not too loudly so no one could hear except him.

Dragon

Poppy was up early to build the fire in the clearing behind the house. The leaf-crackling air made a morning to remind you that summer was gone. Poppy wore his light winter jacket and leather gloves and kept moving. Doc and Charles had dug a small pit the night before and stacked split chestnut oak and kindling nearby. When the fire was ready, they carried the copper kettle out from the cellar and eased it onto its stand above the fire. A thirty-gallon kettle, awkward for two people. Charles said:

— Watch your back.

Doc didn't mention that it was Charles who had thrown his back out last year.

Doc accepted a cup of coffee from Eva, and Leah poured a gallon of cider into the kettle. Then Rosa appeared with the first pan of apples. She dumped them into the kettle, kissed Poppy's cheek, and returned to the kitchen. A pair of mourning doves cooed as the sun rose over the Blue Ridge.

Charles poured vinegar over the six-foot hickory stirring paddle, which had been in the family as long as the kettle. Then he handed the paddle to Poppy, who began stirring. Charles gazed into the kettle, blowing warmth into his slender, agile fingers. He and Doc stood across from each other, neither talking. Their tension was evident. Then Charles went inside to get more coffee, and Eva shouldered up to Poppy.

— Can I stir?

— In a minute. Did you bring the pennies?

— Here, she said, holding out ten shiny ones. Why do we

need the pennies?

—To make sure the butter doesn't stick.

—And for luck, Doc said. Let me see this paddle.

He slipped in front of Poppy to keep the stirring continuous. And Eva sprinkled the pennies into the kettle.

Charles came out and dumped in another pan of apples. Then he eased in front of Doc, and the two stirred together for an instant before Doc let go. Charles stirred smoothly. That's how it went, one giving way to another. The apples would be thick and hard to move until they were all in and cooked down.

By late morning several neighbors had arrived, each bringing something for the potluck, and soon there was a table of covered dishes waiting as reward.

The day moved along. Oblivious of time, people came and went, to talk, laugh, stir, listen, watch. Too cold to sit for very long, those who weren't stirring gathered around the pot talking to those who were. Some went inside to help keep the chopped apples coming, dishes cleaned, and jars prepared. The children, running around wildly, were the only ones unaware of the cold, and they shrieked with laughter.

By the time Billy's dad dropped him off it was late afternoon. Charles spotted him walking up from the road and called:

—Show up late, you gotta work twice as hard! Come on over; let's see what you're made of.

Billy nodded to Eva, who was pleased to see him, then he went over to the kettle for a stirring lesson.

Edmund arrived soon after. As Doc's former mentor, Edmund had been coming to family gatherings for years. Today dark circles hung around his burnt umber eyes. Most assumed the economy fueled his fatigue. A few knew what really troubled him and how deep that trouble ran. He was director of the new state mental institution, and his enthusiasm about experimental science threatened to get the best of him. What had started as "wanting to help people" had turned into a crusade to "remove the undesirables." Whether he knew it or not, he was starting to behave like the pack that was putting Hitler in charge of Germany.

Despite his apparent weariness, Edmund took his turn stirring. When he wasn't wielding the paddle he engaged the older ladies in conversations that made them giggle and blush. Their sweetness soothed his nerves.

When everyone agreed that the stirring had become easy, it was time to add the sugar. The butter and sugar simmered another hour until sunset when Charles announced the saucer test and spooned a glob of butter onto the saucer. He raised it above his head, and then turned it upside down. The children held their breaths waiting for the splat of apple butter on Charles' face that never arrived.

—Time for the spices, he said.

Leah handed him vials of clove and cinnamon while Doc stirred. It was the last step before filling the canning jars. Everyone who wasn't inside preparing the jars gathered around the kettle. The fire was now little more than glowing embers and fulfilling warmth.

Many men came to test their wits by solving the riddle but failed and paid with their lives.

Meanwhile the princess Matoaka continued to appear in Chick's dreams. But she was now a thin, despondent shadow of herself. Her dress hung loosely over her youthful contours. Chick assumed she was grieving for the men who had died because they couldn't solve the riddle. He decided to try something new in his meditation before entering sleep. Instead of focusing on what *he* saw the day the golden chief had been captured, he tried to imagine what *Matoaka* would have seen. Where did she go when she left his dream?

He looked down the narrow path through the pines. The angular crested head of a pileated woodpecker undulated across the path and disappeared into the forest. Then in its wake, Matoaka appeared at the water's edge, walking toward her village. Chick followed. She passed laughing children running through the meadow. Young men played drums, and women chanted while they sewed clothing. Chick watched as Matoaka leaned over a village cook pot to smell the simmering corn chowder. Then she picked up some herbs from a nearby basket, crushed them between her fingers, and sprinkled them into the pot. He could see the steam at her lips when she blew on a spoonful before tasting it. Then he woke.

The next night he followed her into the forest again. Events repeated themselves: the woodpecker's undulating flight, Matoaka, the children, the drums, her village, the cook pots, and the herbs and steam as she bent to taste the corn chowder.

He wanted to keep dreaming, but as she straightened from the steaming pot, she and the village disappeared into a dizzying void. Why had he lost his vision? Where had it gone? Where was Matoaka? As he focused his attention, he started to see a sliver of light. He peered into it and saw a small chamber where Matoaka was undressing for sleep. When Chick averted his eyes, he awoke from the vision he was summoning.

The next night, again the events repeated themselves, but as he turned away from Matoaka undressing, he saw Opech entering her chamber. As Opech neared Matoaka, he turned and seemed to look directly at Chick. But how could he? Chick reassured himself that Opech must be trying to locate Matoaka's guards.

Then to Chick's horror he saw Opech, agile as a wildcat, grab Matoaka. He bound her hands and mouth, tossed her over his shoulder. She kicked the air futilely as he hurried into the forest. Chick followed. Opech moved quickly, occasionally looking back, but no one from the village followed. It took all of Chick's attention to keep up with Opech and Matoaka. And eventually he lost them.

He stopped, not knowing which way to turn. The thick forest wrapped around him. A scream pierced the air, and he heard strange noises rising from deep shadows. Then the forest went quiet except for the distant sound of someone sobbing. Chick strained to see, but he knew now that he had lost control of his dream, and he fell into a blind sleep.

The next night, dreaming again, he was back in the Powhatan village, in the chamber where Opech recited the riddle to each of Matoaka's suitors. He listened as Opech spoke proudly. Then he sat up in a cold sweat. He had heard the secret riddle!

For several days he puzzled over the riddle and what he'd learned about Opech from his dream. It hurt him to imagine the abduction again, knowing he could do nothing about it. But it helped him solve the riddle.

Now he needed a way to use his knowledge. Revealing the solution would only expose such unthinkable crimes that the suggestion itself would condemn him, as the riddle also implied. He felt certain that if he offered the solution himself, he wouldn't leave Wahun's village alive. He needed a plan that Opech would not anticipate.

He would unveil the riddle and its vile roots to Talutah. Chick knew Talutah loved the princess but didn't know that Wahun had intended to propose a marriage between Matoaka and Talutah. If Talutah could disclose the meaning of the riddle to Wahun in secret, then Matoaka, though it would pain her to speak of it, could confirm the riddle's solution. Talutah might have enough time to marry the princess in private and take her far enough away that Opech could not reach her.

Talutah agreed to the plan and accompanied Chick to Wahun's village. But Wahun was unable to meet with them. He had become very ill, as had Matoaka.

Chick feared the worst if the princess remained in the village. Fortunately, one of Matoaka's closest friends who knew and trusted Chick agreed to take him to her. Chick found her weak but able to walk, and when he told her Talutah was waiting at the edge of the village to help her, she agreed to accompany Chick and Talutah back to the golden ones' village. Matoaka sent word to her father that she was seeking a medicine for his illness. Soon after, Talutah kept his promise to protect her and took the princess on a ship across the ocean.

Meanwhile Chick now knew, deep in his heart, that he was being watched in his dreams, no doubt by Opech. He tried to locate Opech in his dreams but could not.

Then one night, Chick decided he must reveal the truth about Opech to Wahun. He didn't know how he would convince him of Opech's treachery, but he had to try.

The next morning he woke to find a messenger waiting at his hut. The message came from Opech, an ultimatum: leave immediately or your entire village will be massacred as a punishment for your involvement in Matoaka's capture. Chick had been charged with treason and would be arrested at sunset.

Opech had been trading with the golden ones, who hadn't realized that all the while he was stealing their weapons. Chick knew the Chickahominy would lose many men if they tried to resist. He decided he must go immediately to Wahun and tell him what he knew. But he didn't get there, meeting on the road the spirit of Wahun, who had died in the night. The spirit told Chick to flee and advised him to put a loyal friend in charge of the village. Wahun's spirit would stay as long as he could to help keep the tribe safe.

We listened to the next segment of Poppy's story while we ate our late supper of vegetable chowder, cornbread, and butternut squash pie. Afterward Billy's dad picked him up, but some folks lingered. I was tired but didn't want to be alone, so I went outside and found a spot on the steps in front of Poppy. Others settled on the porch or on quilts near the fire. Charles had built it back up to take off the chill, and the crackle of wood and warmth mesmerized our eyes, tired from a day spent outside in the sun. In the kitchen, one hundred and eighty-two pints of apple butter lined the table and counter tops, face down, sealing.

Nathaniel tuned his banjo and showed Charles a melody. Charles watched methodically, his ears doing most of the seeing, then picked up his guitar and repeated the melody. Nathaniel grinned his approval.

Several people chuckled when Nathaniel brought the

melody back in double time. He can really pick it. Then Floyd brought out his fiddle, and they eased into steady synchrony. In a few minutes, the three set off on a sweet version of that old tragic one, "Oh, the Wind and Rain." I tapped my foot to the beat. Then Mama and Rosa began to sing:

> There were two sisters of county Clare,
> Oh, the wind and the rain
> One was dark and the other was fair,
> Oh, the dreadful wind and rain

I rested my head on Poppy's knees, and he stroked my hair. Billy'd only left a short while ago, but I missed him already. I wondered if I'd keep missing him the rest of my life.

> And they both had a love of the miller's son,
> Oh, the wind and the rain
> But he was fond of the fairer one,
> Oh, the dreadful wind and rain

> So she pushed her into the river to drown
> Oh, the wind and the rain
> Watched her as she floated down
> Oh, the dreadful wind and rain

When they took a break from the verses, Mama watched Rosa intently. Eyes closed, Rosa leaned her head back and sang astral notes, bringing them from somewhere far away, blending in and out of the melody. When she opened her eyes again she looked at Mama.

Floyd brought the jug to Poppy, who thanked him and took a sip. When he sighed deeply, I could smell the whisky on his breath.

The musicians reeled into an instrumental jam. Low voices took over the night. Mama came and sat next to me.

I don't think anyone else had noticed him when I saw Edmund staggering out of the shadows. I'd assumed he'd left.

He'd started early on the jug, and I hadn't seen him at supper. But there he was, his eyes set on Doc. The music stopped as if by its own volition, and Edmund began to sing:

> Oh what is this, I cannot see
> An icy hand takes hold on me?
> Oh I am death, that none can excel;
> I open the gates to heaven and hell.

Cold silence returned his wavering melody, and he teetered a kind of salute.

> Farewell, farewell, to all farewell;
> My doom is fixed, I'm summoned to hell.
> As long as God in heaven shall dwell,
> My soul, my soul, shall scream in hell.

Long after he'd staggered back into the night, those last notes still rang in my ears.

Serpent

A picket fence enclosed a small cemetery at the edge of the woods two miles above the farm. In the right light, in the right mind, you could see spirits congregating in the shadows. The small whiteboard church on the hill shone brightly. Rosa told Poppy and Eva to go on up while she tended the family graves.

It was warm, and the snake was out early. Eva jumped before she saw it, her reaction a half-second faster than thinking allowed. She stood transfixed. Poppy moved quickly, silently, easing her back a few steps until she was clear of striking range, the snake now coiled and rattling.

—You needn't worry about this one, Poppy said.

—Why?

—Because it's in front of the church.

Timber rattler, dark phase, fourteen, maybe sixteen rattles. Happened by the church by chance some might say. Others would suspect it had another purpose, perhaps to become a good rattle in a mandolin. But, no, this rattler wasn't bound for a musical instrument.

Poppy recognized one of the men standing at the bottom of the steps as the evangelist from a Holiness Church in Jolo, West Virginia. He led a serpent handling congregation in that hard luck mining town, and a couple carloads of his followers had come with him for a revival, probably hoping to convert a few of the mountain people here. But these were farmers not miners; they were not accustomed to taking eerie risks such as traveling into the somber reaches of the mountain's interior. Many believed in faith healing, but they didn't relish handling snakes. The evangelist said:

—You would not believe how the power of the Lord comes over you when you hold a snake in your hands. The world stops. And there's just you, with nothing around you but silence.

—Sounds like dying, Poppy said.

—No, sir. Just the opposite.

One of the younger men jogged to his car and came back with a burlap bag. He handed it to an older man who had moved closer to the snake, watching it and speaking softly.

Rosa had seen the commotion and came to where Eva was staring, spellbound, and said:

—You all right?

—Yes. But do you smell that?

—What?

—Cucumbers.

—Well, that's what some say rattlers smell like.

—What'll they do to it?

—The rattler? Take it back to West Virginia, feed it, take care of it.

—They won't kill it?

—No. The snake is part of their religion.

—Religion? Like a church?

—Sure. It's part of their beliefs. Based on their interpretation of the Bible.

The rattling intensified as the older man reached forward. Then in a lightning quick movement, he snapped his thumb and finger just behind the snake's head. He held the snake in the air while it writhed and wound around his arm.

Rosa said:

—Some folks will take that as a sign.

—I expect so, Poppy said.

—It does seem strange that a big rattler happened to appear this morning.

—A coincidence? Eva asked. But I thought you said there were no coincidences, Poppy.

—And I meant what I said. It's just that sometimes you must

contemplate events a while before you understand why they are not coincidences.

—But ...

—We'll talk about it later if you want. Look there, it's your cousin.

The bouncing brunette skipping toward them was a granddaughter of one of Rosa's sisters. Eva ran to meet her. No doubt they would want to watch the men and the snake, and Poppy knew better than to discourage curiosity. He climbed the steps to the sanctuary while Rosa started down the stairs to the basement Sunday School room. She called to the girls, who were standing hand in hand, eyes glued to the scene.

—Hurry here, you two. I'll need your help with the young'ens.

Upstairs the organist was pumping her hands and feet in solid rhythms while her body swayed in a circular motion. A handful of men stood in front of the first pew speaking louder than one would expect. Floyd motioned to Poppy, who stepped closer and listened.

—It's Edmund's way of taking control. He only comes back up the holler when he wants something.

—Nah, he's just being neighborly. Looking out for the rest of us.

—Neighborly is fine, but something isn't right about those men he brought. You can feel it.

Floyd turned to Poppy:

—What do you say, Mr. Walton?

Several others turned as well.

—Neighborly is fine. If a church can't open its doors, then who can?

—And you trust Edmund?

—I didn't say that. But I'll reserve judgment until all the evidence is in.

—He's making quite a commotion in town recruiting for his new hospital.

Poppy knew that Edmund had been insisting that Floyd's sister commit her teenage daughter for treatment. Doc had examined her as well but had found no evidence that she was unstable or insane. And in Doc's opinion, to describe anyone as insane was a poor and insufficient way of characterizing a person. Consider the conclusions you jumped to. But Edmund could be convincing, persuading parents that they would be negligent to leave their children's "abnormal" conditions untreated.

Poppy said:

—Shouldn't we get the morning service started? When those West Virginians come in, we don't want to look uncivilized.

The men found their places in the pews, and Reverend Koiner stepped to the pulpit, Bible in hand. The West Virginians were sitting and standing together in the back. Edmund walked in a minute later, nodding to the newcomers, and took a seat down front.

As was the custom after service, the congregation convened for lunch. The women spread out their prepared dishes on a long table between two tall maples behind the church. Poppy surveyed the group, reflecting on how far people had traveled to be together. Many had walked several miles and would continue to make their journey as long as they were able.

The West Virginians walked up with Edmund, whose heaviness from the day before had lifted, his demeanor wiped clean. His dark gray felt fedora matched his spotless suit and tie. He even wore the spectacles he normally reserved for office work. Offering a gentle nod, he said to Poppy:

—Fine day isn't it, Mr. Walton?

—A little warm. But the Lord works in his own way.

—No doubt he does, Mr. Walton. No doubt he does.

Of course the Mr. Walton formality was just a masquerade. Edmund knew Poppy's name as well as he knew his own. But he also knew that things would never be the same between them.

Poppy was acquainted with Edmund's "Vision for a Brighter

World." He had heard Edmund argue for a purer race, one better suited to solve the world's problems. Edmund's arguments fed on the fear that springs from hard times. *We must isolate our weaknesses and remove them.* Edmund had become powerful. The affluent, the insecure sought him. But the rural communities had resisted. For them, hardship was a way of life: failed crops, sick livestock, and always more children on the way.

In the fall of 1933, the resonance from the stock market meltdown sounded the dimmest economy yet: record unemployment, world-wide wealth at rock bottom. After four straight years: think about what it can do to the psyche. And while the country people's subsistence farming could buffer them from large-scale economic tides, the drought would determine their lives. And the drought held sway for the fourth year in a row. Four years of shallower pockets, drier soils. Hope stretched thinner than the brittle ghost of a snake, sloughed off by a soul who'd outgrown his skin.

Yet the church family gathered around the serving table, and the Reverend gave a prayer of thanks.

—God of countless names, your handiwork is spread before us …

The youth took their plates and sat beneath the maples, far enough away to entertain their own topics of interest. The adults sat on benches near the table.

When Edmund saw that everyone had been served, he stood.

—I'd like to say a little something. If y'all don't mind.

The men and women politely curtailed their conversations and turned their attention to Edmund.

—I look around me here today and see good people. Good people who've known no life but that of hard work and trust in the Lord. And we thank the Lord for his blessings upon us.

—Praise God, Amen, the involuntary voices answered him.

—But I say you've been dealt more than your share of hardship in this life. They say the times are changing. But we people in this poor county can't just stand around and *wait* for the changes to trickle down while things fall apart in the meantime. I say y'all've been waiting long enough. You deserve better.

People looked at each other hesitantly, not used to a post-service sermon.

—Now I see you come to the Lord with sickness and trials. And the people in town come to see me. You would too if you all didn't have a crush on that young buck, Doc Walton. (*Edmund chuckled.*) Now where is the fine doctor today? Well, no matter. You're here, I'm here, because we believe in the good Lord. We believe He has a plan for us. All of us. I know you need to find solutions to your tribulations, and I'm happy to say I've found it for you: a solution. I've been working hard for the better part of my career, with scientists around the country, to find cures for those among the flock whose physical sufferings stem from something deep inside them, something they can't control on their own. But we can. You may not even realize that they are so afflicted. But boy, you'll know it, and feel that relief, when your burdens are lifted.

A few nods of assent from the group while others expressed mistrust with crossed arms or shifting feet.

—I came up here today to tell you all that we townspeople have a vision for every one of you. A new way of seeing how things are. Yes, yes I know that you sometimes don't appreciate us "townies," but we're not that different from you. No. We're just like you. We want prosperity same as you. We want to be able to support our families same as you. We want what's right same as you. And that's why I'm pleased to tell you today that we're opening a new hospital for all!

Edmund welcomed the sincere attention he read in the eyes focused on him.

—A new hospital, the finest in the state, one that will help the less fortunate among us have a home, a place where their lives can be improved through the wonders of modern medicine. And for that, I say *Hallelujah.*

But his wonders of modern medicine only produced stoned faces. The word "hospital" had its positive connotation, but most of these people had no idea what Edmund's hospital was about since no one spoke openly about procedures such as compulsory sterilization for the mentally ill. But Poppy knew. And Doc knew what these new experimental institutions, steeped in eugenics theory, would lead to. Still, Poppy held his tongue. He knew that was the best choice for protecting his kin. He tried to convince himself that nothing would come of Edmund's speech today. But later, when folks were home wrestling with their own afflictions they'd start to think Edmund might be right, that we needed to put our "mentally unfortunates," as he'd heard Edmund call them, in a hospital for their own good. Doc knew better. Poppy knew better. But how do you reassure people who see no way out?

—So, Edmund said, the unfortunate sons and daughters among us need our help. It's not their fault that their *genetics* predispose them to certain limitations. At the hospital, we'll diagnose their inadequacies and provide them with the best care imaginable.

Whisperings in the crowd suggested interest.

—For as long as necessary, he added. We're here for the long run, building a better society.

Someone said:

—How you gonna pay for it?

—My friends, this hospital will be an institution supported by the state itself. The most affluent and intelligent individuals across our fine country have already demonstrated their support with generous gifts and donations.

—It won't cost us anything?

—Not a penny. We want to ensure that your family has the best life possible. What could be more important than helping your own flesh and blood? Help them, you help yourselves. Isn't that right?

—Hallelujah, someone said.

But the Reverend grimaced, his body's tension expressed in his arms held straight along his side, terminated in tight fists.

—Edmund, are you telling these people the truth? About that new hospital of yours?

—Why, Reverend, do you insinuate I would mislead these good people? We are in this together aren't we? We want to make the world a brighter place to live in, don't we?

Poppy, Rosa, and Eva were quiet as they walked home, focusing on the two steep miles.

The woods had grown lighter with the canopy of leaves trading in their dense emerald attire for garments of gold and crimson, one by one taking the leap of faith, as if lured down by the rising aromas of those who had gone before.

Rosa slipped her arm around Poppy's waist. Trailing a few steps behind, Eva broke the silence:

—I wouldn't be any trouble (*she eased the words out*) if I stayed with you. At least until the end of the school year.

Rosa and Poppy stopped and turned. Eva continued, more quickly:

—I'm in the middle of everything right now. And this way Doc and Mama could get settled in, and I could start off fresh, next year, in Colorado.

Rosa looked at Poppy who said:

—Your parents would miss you terribly if you stayed here.

—But I'll miss you terribly.

—And we'll miss you. Your father wants to make a new beginning. Leaving you behind would make it harder than it already is for him.

—Then maybe we should just stay.

Poppy inhaled slowly, exhaled, said:

—There's nothing in the world we want more than to have you with us, but you will be—

—With you in memories. I know. But I want to be with you here, like now.

Her face was distraught, on the verge of tears. Poppy pulled her to him and said:

—Memory, my darling, is more than a scrapbook of images.

SERPENT

Then I was
and wasn't
on the train

floating
above the tracks
with leaves

swirling around me
I could see
what was before us

before we came
to the creek
I was suddenly certain

I was
and I wasn't alone
a hand caressed

my face and arms
lifted me above
the water as we crossed

to the far bank
where leaves now
sparkled like diamonds

and I was
and wasn't
on the train.

That much
I know
so far.

With Wahun's spirit advising him, Chick greeted the morning near the confluence of the Chickahominy and the Sacred River. While he swam toward the far shore, he considered how he could protect his people. Although the thought of leaving his home hurt deeply, he knew he must go. He knew his people were strong and would survive without his being near them. And he would be with them in spirit. Their safety depended on diverting attention away from themselves.

By the time he was mid-river, he had imagined a crew of his most loyal companions, his course, and his canoes laden with food and supplies. He knew what he would do. He needed to get above the Falls and into the misty mountains where Opech and the Powhatans had little influence. His canoes would need four days to get above the Falls, another seven to reach the Great Bend in the river, four days to the Hill City, and two days to reach Two Rivers where Chick knew he'd be safe in the foothills of the Blue Ridge.

Two Rivers was ruled jointly by chief Manki and his wife Mihani. They ruled as one, just as the two rivers in their territory joined to become the Sacred River. Their people called them Manki and Mihani because these names meant husband and wife, signifying their partnership. Whenever one had a strong feeling regarding the direction of the people, the other respected the presentiment.

As he imagined Manki and Mihani greeting him from the riverbank at Two Rivers, Chick felt heavyhearted and wondered why. What was it about Two Rivers that worried his spirit? The news that had come down the river last year suggested that the mountain people were at peace and in good health. He recalled Two Rivers as a thriving village. But as he looked harder in his mind, he made out a thin, haggard person standing at the river's edge. So he decided to load extra canoes with food and supplies to prepare for the unknown.

Chick trotted along the riverbank to where his good friend was waiting.

—Winkapew, Chick said, you are my true and loyal friend. Send word to each of the seven villages along the Chickahominy that I have dreamt. Ask each of them to send four men with canoes loaded with squash and ground corn. It will be our gift to Manki and Mihani and the people of Two Rivers. Have the men prepare for a three-week journey, or longer.

By sunset, the group was casting off from the mouth of the Chickahominy and starting up the Sacred River. The men stood with long pine poles, guiding the canoes against the current.

Three days later they made camp just below the Falls. The next day they strapped baskets of squash and corn to their backs and carried them up the steep slope. A few men remained to guard the supplies and make a high camp. The rest returned to portage their canoes. By nightfall, exhausted, they sat around the campfire, eating and drinking, and imagining their loved ones downriver.

The next morning they continued upriver. The Falls fell behind them. Chick's scouts alerted the small Powhatan villages along the way that a priest was passing through. The Chickahominy and Powhatan peoples were at peace with each other, so Chick's journey went smoothly. The river was low, and the canoes moved swiftly. Soon, they were in Two Rivers where Manki and Mihani met them at the shore.

—You are a gift sent from the spirits of the sky, Mihani said.

—To whom we have been praying, Manki added, embracing his wife. But how did you know?

Twins

*P*oppy was knee-deep in the tailrace, bolting a section of the wheel, when Nathaniel walked out.

— Mr. Poppy. Fine morning ain't it?

— Yes, it is. Time for your breakfast? Say hello to your missus for me.

— Yes sir, I will, and I'll tell her you'll be coming up for one of her hoecakes later.

— You think I need fattening?

— No sir, you look fine enough. But you can always use one of Naomi's hoecakes with apple butter. Missus Rosa won't mind. And I hear she and Missus Leah are going to town this morning.

— All right then. I'll come up as soon as I finish this wheel.

— You need some help with that?

— I'll manage. You go on to your breakfast. Save me a cup a' coffee.

Nathaniel crossed the pasture and climbed the hill. He starts the mill early by himself. Only after someone has arrived to take over the wheel does he return to his cabin for his breakfast. Each morning Poppy listens for the wheel turning, his alarm clock. His brother, Abe, had hired Nathaniel when Charles and Doc went to the War. After Abe died, Nathaniel supervised the mill, Poppy the farm. They helped each other.

Nathaniel married Naomi during the War. Solid as a rock, she could carry as many sacks of grain as any man. The children must have felt light after that, and they had four young girls before they knew it. Two of them attended that little school on the river. One room, pot belly stove. Nathaniel was proud that he was able to send them to school; many families had no choice but to keep their kids at home to help with the work.

The women on the farm (Iris, Rosa, Naomi, Katie) like women everywhere had kept their families together while men fought far from home. Poppy's mother Iris had made certain the family stayed in good health. She was known throughout that part of Virginia as a healer. She was body and spirit, and everyone in the family knew it was her magic that had pulled them through hard times.

Rosa fed them, able to stir a stew from nearly bare cupboards. Her family had lived up the holler for as long as she knew, and they were used to living on little. Before Katie began to fail, more noticeably after her husband Abe died, she kept everyone on their toes despite her bad memory. And sweet Lily, God rest her soul, wasn't with them long.

Charles and Doc had both seen too much death and insanity during the War, but they had responded differently. Doc could no longer enjoy the peacefulness of the farm, while the farm and the mountains had become Charles' refuge. Doc started a medical practice near town. Charles became Nathaniel's partner in the mill.

Although Doc didn't spend much time at the mill he had gone there later that morning to see Charles. Poppy was still working outside when he heard the brothers arguing.

— You didn't even discuss the move with me.

— And what good would that have done, Charles?

— There are ways to handle this.

Seeing Doc standing there by the window shaking his head, Poppy was reminded of the times when he and Abe had argued about how to run the farm.

Charles said:

— You think you can just run away from all this? It'll never end. You won't outrun it.

— It will. He's not after you. I'm the one who's threatening his business.

— Business? If you can call it that. Is that what they're doing? I thought doctors healed people.

—Not always.

—You're damn right, not always. You know what some of them do. And you're not like them. And if you think Ave and Iris are safe …

Doc cut him off with a wave.

—If I stay, and he does what he says, he'll take the mill down, and you know it. His people will spread the word, and we'll be lucky to have any customers from town. And they're the ones with capital. Nathaniel is hard enough for the town folks to bear already.

—Because he's a black man. Don't worry; we'll be fine. People need flour. The people out here will still come to us.

—All I'm saying is we need to fight this one without hurting our own people. He's got me pinned.

—How? Why can't you stand up for yourself?

—Look. Just because you come home with a black eye every other week doesn't make you a brave man. Just a fighter. I'm fighting this my own way. Hell, it's your secret I'm keeping.

The men stood in silence. Then Doc looked down and said:

—I didn't mean to put it like that.

—Should've left when I had the chance.

—Charles, the family needs you here. What's done is done. And we can all live with it if you let me handle this my way.

—You know it's my mistake that got us here.

—Not yours. Not a mistake at all. Ours, if anything. She was not a mistake. She was a gift; we all know that. But fighting this won't remedy what's already happened. It will cause us all harm. I made my decision long ago when I signed that first paper. I lied then to keep them safe. And now I have to leave to keep them safe.

—You know what you did was right.

—I do. And I'll keep doing what I think is right by protecting what I believe in.

—Even if it means leaving your home?

Doc turned his head and exhaled, then said:

—If it leaves my home safe for the rest of my family.

TWINS

The conductor walks the aisle chanting:

—Chicago. Next stop, Chi-ca-go. Arriving in fifteen minutes. Passengers connecting to Madison, board in the bus terminal to your right. Your bags will be beside the train. Chi-ca-go. Next stop.

My heart beats faster. Chicago, the World's Fair! I can't wait to send Billy a postcard. Then I feel Doc's hand on my shoulder.

—When we get to the station stay close to your mother. It's a big place, and I don't want you to get lost.

He hands me a flyer: *Sky Ride: Supreme Thrill of the Century of Progress World's Fair.*

But wait! Below us, a river … it must be the Chicago! With a park on one side and big weeping willows.

Then before I know it, we're coming through rail yards, tracks upon tracks upon tracks, and other passengers are suddenly rising from their seats, getting their bags, talking, urgent to get up or down the aisle.

I stay where I am and try to think fast because I don't have much time to write before we get to Chicago's Union Station. Billy will be excited to hear about everything we'll learn. It's too bad we can't play Invisible Universe now. But I need to focus on the Monday after Apple Butter weekend, October 23rd. When you're moving so fast it's easy to lose track.

Then something happened that changed everything.

Billy's dad picked him up from school. The college orchestra was performing a Mozart concerto that evening, and his dad was taking him to hear it. Billy's dad is cultural. Billy says they're going to take the train to New York at Christmas to see Billie Holiday. Billy's dad says she's going to be a big jazz star when she's older. But she's already eighteen, Billy said, and that's old enough for most things. He'd better send me a postcard.

I walked home alone. After I finished my homework, Kleela and I climbed to the lookout. The farm in twilight expanded into a magenta and mauve landscape. An artist's. What's it like to paint? I've drawn a little, but I don't have enough talent. They say geniuses are born that way, or something like that.

I leaned back against one of my favorite perches (you know, the rocks have shelves, benches, seats, thrones, nooks, whatever you have a mind for). I let my thoughts drift: along the ridge, down the slope, along the deer trail, past the blackberry bushes, until I reached the seep. I stopped there and splashed water on my face. Yellow sword-shaped leaves dropped into the water and slid over mossy rocks.

And that's when I heard the thrush, bringing me back to the present. *E-o-ah, E-o-ah*, she sang. I listened and smiled, wondering if Ave would appear. I tried to be still, but trying can make it harder. I silently begged Kleela not to bark. I kept my eyes closed to stop my fidgeting and listened. She was closer now. *E-o-ah, E-o-ah*, she called high in the branches. Then I heard a footfall. It wasn't Kleela because I could hear her breathing near me. *E-o-ah, E-o-ah*. I wanted to open my eyes so badly, but I was afraid that would ruin everything.

I pictured her in front of me: in a dark red dress, wearing red and white beads, auburn hair loose and long, pale fingers reaching toward me, big brownish-green eyes looking into mine. I was so focused on imagining the details that I barely noticed the song moving above and behind me. She must have been perched on the rock when she touched my left shoulder. I almost flinched but didn't, nor did I open my eyes. Her long fingers slid down my arm with a lightness. I turned my head, and her fingers stopped. Then she whistled *E-o-ah* and flew. I opened my eyes, my heart pounding.

Chick remained in Two Rivers with his new friends for one cycle of the moon. The corn he brought restored their people who had grown weary and sick. That fall of 1609, the drought was widespread. Leaves wilted, crinkled, dropped, tired and thirsty. Men and women took their children into cooler, higher country. Birds vanished.

Chick liked the people in Two Rivers and was beginning to think he need not travel farther when a short and hurried message arrived from Winkapew:

> Move quickly
> Opech isn't far behind you.
> You don't have enough warriors
> to confront him.

Chick sent most of his men back to their families on the Chickahominy. He knew Opech was interested only in him. His men would be safer downriver. With only three canoes Chick set out immediately, following the mountains north.

Then abruptly, dark winds blew. The first drops of rain were welcome, but soon rain and hail became a tempest pounding parched soil into muddy clay that gushed into the river. Chick and his men looked for a landing, but the banks were too steep. A tree fell. Logs and branches spun in the raging rapids. A wave rushing downriver capsized the first canoe, then the second and the third. Men and boats swirled like leaves.

Later, not knowing how, Chick pulled himself ashore, gasping. He crawled the short stretch his muddled mind would allow him and collapsed under the long, protective branches of a pine. Rain fell. He burrowed himself deeper into the pine needles.

Voices vibrated through his empty dark sleep, clashing in his ears. Strange water rushed just out of reach, and his mouth was drier than he could remember. He fell in and out of sleep and finally awoke in a place and time he didn't recognize. He tried to get up, his vision blurry, but reaching for what he thought was a root, he recoiled in pain. He cried out, certain he was dying, then lost consciousness, falling into a silent white asleep.

When he awoke again, he smelled the smoke of simmering wet wood. He was lying near two men who squatted next to a small fire. One drank from an animal skin and passed it to the other. Chick smelled, then saw, fish stacked neatly. His hand was bandaged with leaves. He was naked, wrapped in a blanket.

—Where am I? he mumbled.

The fisherman said:

—South of the great village of Three Sisters, the land of good chief Konspewa.

Konspewa, Chick thought, *he who remembers*. He had heard of this chief who developed and practiced great memory arts. Then Chick, remembering his group, said:

—My men? Where are they?

—If you mean the ones in the other canoes, one of us looks for them. But you shouldn't raise your hopes. You were foolish to be on the river last night.

—There's always hope.

—As you will, stranger. Who are you?

—Chickacawcaw, a priest of my tribe, the Chickahominy, downriver, near the mouth of the Sacred River.

A second fisherman looked up from his work.

—A priest? A drowned rabbit is more like it.

Chick tried to sit up. But the first fisherman said:

—Rest where you are. If you say you're a priest, we believe you. We don't have time for debate. As soon as our friend returns, we're leaving for Three Sisters, where the festival starts today. Young men from all the nearby villages are coming to compete for Konspewa's daughter's hand in marriage.

—Aye, the other said. She's called Tesihiyan, body of sleep, because she is so at ease, just seeing her will lull you. It will be a feast for the eyes.

—Yes, the first said, a feast for the eyes. But she was so named because she slept soundly as a baby.

The two were still debating the origin of her name when the third fisherman arrived.

—I found no sign of your party, he said. Only this spear along the bank.

—My spear! Chick cried out. The spear of my father. It has his mark.

The sight of the spear renewed Chick's strength, and he stood to face the fisherman.

—He gave it to me. I would say you should keep it for the kindness you've shown me. And you found it, but I swear if you allow me to go with you to Three Sisters, I will compete at your festival and pay you back many times over for your kindness.

The first fisherman chuckled.

—If not for us, you'd already be dead. That was a moccasin that bit you.

Chick looked at his hand.

—If you trust me, you won't regret it.

The two seated fishermen looked at their friend with the spear and at Chick. The first said to the third:

—It's up to you.

The one with the spear looked at Chick.

—It's an old spear. Let him have it. I can make better myself.

With that he sat, taking cooked fish offered by the second fisherman who said:

—You'll need more than a blanket, priest.

And he reached into his bag and tossed Chick dry clothing.

Deer

*J*hold Mama's hand as we deboard the train at Chicago's Grand Union Station. Mama has our overnight bag, and I have my notebook. I think about my last days at the farm. Poppy said I can recall everything that happens if I practice *remembering* and write what I remember in my notebook.

While Mama and I wait outside, Doc unloads our trunks and puts them into a storage compartment in the station. Large posters, many of them taller than I am, advertise the World's Fair. My favorite is *A Century of Progress*: a woman in a flowing robe stands on a globe, raising her arms. She's surrounded by statues, buildings, planes, skyscrapers, and a rainbow.

People buzz by us, rushing to the Fair, while others sit quietly, on chairs and benches, in no hurry to go anywhere.

Mama seems at ease. She grew up riding trains.

—Does this look like Austria, Mama?

—No. But seeing people rushing around does remind me of the cities near my Austrian home.

—You have a lot of homes.

—I guess so, a few. But home, like they say, is where your heart is.

I thought about that. I remembered her stories about Europe where Mama said people ride trains everywhere. She met Doc in the Paris train station. She was alone. She had tried to convince her family to leave Austria with her. But they wouldn't; it had been *home* all their lives. But Mama knew she had to leave. She would never have met Doc if she hadn't.

—All set, Doc says, smoothing my hair and kissing Mama's

cheek. We'll pick up our trunks tomorrow afternoon when we catch the *Chief*.

Doc checks us into a hotel. We shower, change, eat sandwiches, and walk to the World's Fair.

I almost can't believe it. I hear festive music coming from blocks away, and the entrance swarms with people. Vendors sell popcorn and cotton candy, shirts, bags, buttons, who knows what all. But dozens of men off to one side are lined up, holding their hats in their hands. A man in a worn brown coat says to Doc:

—Spare change, mister?

Doc hands him a coin, apologizes to the man standing beside him, and guides us toward a ticket window. It costs a dollar and twenty five cents to get in. We walk under the arch with U.S. flags flapping above us and then down an entire street of flags. It feels like the Fourth of July. A brass band comes into view. But then I remember the men lined up outside. I wonder what that means. It was like this in Indianapolis too. I try not to think about it.

—Science finds, industry applies, and man conforms, Doc recites the World's Fair motto, looking at me quizzingly. Only conform to the world's currents if they conform to yours, not the other way around.

We pass a building that could be a theater.

—Infant Incubators? I ask, reading the playbill. With living babies?

—That may be, Doc says, shaking his head. You wouldn't guess that even with incubators the United States has one of the highest infant death rates.

—Problems everywhere, Mama says.

When we stop to check a map, Doc says:

—Let's start with the Sky Ride. From there we can see the entire park, 427 acres. Bigger than the farm. We'll get oriented.

—Can we go up to the telescopes? I ask.

—I'd like that, Mama says. It'll be like the Eiffel Tower.

She smiles at Doc, and I wonder if they've been there together. Doc says:

—Did you know the Eiffel Tower was built for a world's fair too?

We pass building after building, propelled into motion by the tide of people, more than I've seen in all my life.

Mama says:

—Look, it's the new Singer.

The sewing machine's bright aluminum glimmers in the sunlight.

—Singer Featherweight, Doc reads.

—It must be light as a feather. Or at least a lot lighter than my old cast-iron Sewhandy.

—Perhaps it's a good thing we left it behind? Doc says. Maybe these Featherweights will make it to Colorado before long.

Brightly colored quilts wave in the breeze, and Mama steps closely to examine the stitching. One quilt has a white-tailed deer bounding into the forest. Its tail poofs from the quilt, but the rest of its body disappears into the trees. Doc reads the label pinned to the bottom corner:

—Little Deer, a collaborative quilt by the South River Friends of Bedford. That's close to home.

—South River, Mama says. I've met some of them. They started a co-op to support the regional textile industry. They've helped a lot of small mills.

—I wonder how many people here in Chicago know about Little Deer, Doc says. You remember it, don't you Eva?

—Sure, I say as we walk on. Long ago, the people of Turtle Island prospered, and they eventually learned to use weapons like spears and bows and arrows. This allowed them to kill many more animals than they needed. They no longer respected or thanked the animals they killed. At the rate they were killing, the animals feared there would be none of them left. They gathered in the woods to decide what to do. At first, some of the animals thought they could fight back. But the problems with killing people just because they were trying to kill you became obvious. They needed a better plan. That's when Little Deer came into the story. The animals decided Little Deer would whisper into the ears of all the hunters, telling them that they must respect the animals they hunted. They must ask the animals for permission to hunt them and thank the animal spirits afterward. Any hunter who was disrespectful would be crippled.

—I think there's truth to that legend, Doc says. And a disrespectful hunter can be physically or mentally crippled.

—Is that what the story means?

—What do you think?

Mama says:

—Reckless killing kills the soul of the hunter.

People are everywhere, on both sides, above us, in front and behind. I've never seen so many in one place. I hold Mama's hand. Doc will find the way to the Sky Ride; it can't be any harder than finding Billy's haunted cabin.

That Tuesday, Billy and I sat together near the front of the bus. He leaned toward me and whispered:

—What do you know about a haunted cabin in the woods behind my house?

—What?

—A haunted cabin. Or are the guys pulling my leg?

I laughed. Billy had bought a tale about a haunted cabin.

—Maybe you're just afraid to go see it?

—Billy, I'm sure there's no haunted cabin up there. You can't believe everything people tell you.

—Then why should I believe you?

I rolled my eyes.

—You don't have to.

—Then let's just check it out. You like exploring. Let's be sure *and certain*. There's no harm in looking.

His argument made sense, but I remembered:

—You know snakes are still active. We saw a rattler Sunday.

—You said that was unusual. It'd been drawn to the church or something. And we can watch where we step.

—OK, but we won't find anything.

We dropped off our books at home, crossed Mill Creek, which was running low, and climbed along the edge of the woods until we were above Billy's house. The wind was rising.

— They said it was straight up from here.

— How far up?

— Didn't say. Let's just see where this trail goes.

I didn't see a trail, but I followed Billy, who was enjoying leading the way. I braided my hair to get it out of my face, and we scrambled up between outcrops of smooth white limestone. Tall oaks and rough-barked dogwood sent red and yellow leaves gliding around us. The farm shrank below. Aunt Katie's house and her smokehouse became tiny rectangles. But the Blue Ridge loomed in the distance unaffected.

We reached a bald knoll where we could see down into a ravine. Another ridge rose a few hundred yards away on the other side. We slid into the ravine, then started up a rocky slope toward the ridge. The rocks were smaller and hidden now, and I lost my footing. A sapling kept me from falling. Billy was having a hard time too, a few steps behind me now.

— Are you OK? he said.

— Yes, keep coming. I'm fine.

I thought about the snake at the church. We were heading in the direction of a high valley folks called Dark Hollow. Some said a community of snake handlers lived there. I'd always assumed that was gossip, but when you're in dense woods that you don't know well, the difference between the truth and a tall tale can get jumbled. And I had heard about people who went to town only once a month and women who seldom went at all. So I couldn't really say for sure who might live where.

I stopped to catch my breath and let Billy catch up.

— Maybe we should turn back? I said.

— It's not much farther to the ridge, and from there we'll be able to see where we are. Ridges are smooth on top, right?

But this ridge was not smooth and offered no open views. The woods closed around us. Still, a faint smell, almost sweet, came from somewhere.

— Smell that? Billy asked.

So we tried to follow it and came into an open area of short orchard grass and old tangly pawpaws. Faint wagon wheel ruts curved down into a shallow ravine.

—See, Billy said, I told you. A trail!

—But it's only about an hour before dark. Maybe we should head back?

—Let's go a little way. We still have time.

At first the rutted trail paralleled the slope, and then it dropped abruptly into a narrow valley that turned farther away from the farm. Billy touched my shoulder.

—We don't have to go any farther. I'm just gullible, I guess. And I thought this would be fun.

—This is fun. I don't mind if we don't find anything. Which would prove I was right.

—Then we'll go a little farther?

—I'll follow you.

I wasn't as confident as I pretended to be, but I didn't want to disappoint Billy. We wound through a tangle of wild grape vines and picked a few bunches of shriveling fruit. The sour juice puckered our mouths. We spat seeds as we walked. The trees grew darker and moaned in the cool breeze.

—Did you hear that? Billy said.

—Squirrel?

—Yeah, I guess. I thought I heard footsteps.

I looked back. I heard the squirrel and a vireo singing in a tree above us. What else? I closed my eyes. A creaking. The trees, but also something else, a tapping. Then quiet. My eyes were still closed when Billy touched my arm. It was comforting until I realized he was pulling me back up the trail. I opened my eyes. My stomach churned. My heart beat faster.

—Eva.

Billy's eyes were wide and serious. Then I heard it too; it sounded like a child laughing, high and giddy.

—Let's go, Billy said, urging me up the slope.

I turned again and saw something I'd missed before, the corner of a cabin porch. I heard the giggling again. And I ran. From somewhere behind us, a shot.

—Hunters, I shouted, running. But they can't be shooting at us.

We ran until we were out of breath, not quite to the ridge, no longer following the wagon path we'd come down. Nothing looked right. I was scared, but I had to look back.

—Golly, are we spooked or what? Billy said.

—There was something there.

—I know. I saw it too. Did you see the …

—The what? I heard creepy giggling. And the creaking. And the cabin? Did you see it?

—I saw …

Billy took my hand.

—What else did you see? I said.

—You won't believe me.

—Sure I will.

—You'll say the creaking was the trees. The giggling was a brook. And the—

—What is it?

—Let's keep going.

A little farther, Billy stopped again.

—Don't laugh at me. But I thought I saw something, either a big man or a bear. Really.

—At that cabin?

—He looked huge. I mean it. It wasn't my imagination.

—The place looked abandoned to me.

—I know, I know. But it felt like he—or it—the shadow or whatever, was laughing at us. He seemed to be … shaking, on the porch.

—It sounded like a child to me.

—I know, I know. It's impossible. Come on.

The air was cooler, and the sun had disappeared from our side of the ridge. I heard water running, but I didn't see a creek. We needed something to lift our spirits. I said:

—Let's practice a memory journey.

—What? Oh, OK. Where do we start?

But we didn't get started. As we came around the bend, still below the ridge, we heard a second shot, much closer this time.

Then a grizzly bearded man stepped in front of us, holding a shotgun. He spat.

—What ya'll doin' back here?

—We … Billy started. We didn't mean to … we're just out …

Then through an opening in the woods, I could see a campfire. And the water I'd heard before was flowing through narrow troughs. Two other men stood in the shadows.

—Who sent you up here?

—No one, I said. We're just looking for something.

—What something?

I could see a dark man coming toward us. Tall as I made him out, as he got closer … Yes, I breathed a sigh of relief; it was Nathaniel.

—Eva May, he said, more sternly than usual. And Mr. Billy.

He turned to the other man.

—Put down that gun, soldier. What are you pointin' it at chil'ens for?

—They're grown enough, Nate. Snitches.

Nathaniel stared at the man, who relaxed his shotgun toward the ground.

—You see they don't come back. You better see to 'em.

—Quit your worrying. Get back to work. I'll take these two home.

—That Twenty-first isn't official yet. You know how the sheriff would love to bust us.

—It'll pass. Any day now.

Nathaniel said to us:

—How did you find your way back here? Never mind.

We followed him around an edge of the ridge and down the other side. Then we followed a deer trail that seemed to take the gentlest contours. In a while, Nathaniel started singing, a song I'd heard him sing dozens of times.

> Rabbit in a hole and I ain't got my dog.
> How will I get it? I know.
> *I know* (I whispered in response.)

I'll get me a briar, and I'll twist it in his hair.
That's how I'll get it. I know.
I know.

I know. *I know.*
I know. *I surely know.*
That's how I'll get it, I know.

₰

Chick followed the fishermen to Three Sisters, named for the three crops—beans, corn, and squash—grown there in abundance. It was clear to Chick that the fishermen who found him had powerful medicines he knew nothing about. When he asked about his cure, one said:
—Thank the Great Spirit for your recovery.
The festive atmosphere in Three Sisters surpassed anything Chick had experienced in his native lowlands. The village bustled with people in red, black, yellow, and green. Joyful music intoxicated the air.
They passed lodge after lodge before stopping in a large field encircled by stones. In the heart of the circle, on a stone platform, a chief and his attendants watched contestants file pass. Each contestant introduced himself and bowed to the chief and his beautiful daughter, Tesi, who sat beside him. When it was Chick's turn, he held his bandaged hand behind him and said he was a visitor from the lowlands. Konspewa looked skeptically but as was the custom welcomed him.
Wrestling rings were set up on one end of the field, spear throwing and archery on the other. An obstacle course through the woods included a swim upriver against the current. This had always been the climactic event. Summoning all his strength and more, Chick placed well in all the early events, but the key to his victory was a winning swim. Despite his weakness from the storm, his many years of swimming each morning, a ritual in his

line of priests, made the difference.

At the celebratory feast, Chick was taken by the willingness of the other contestants to accept him. These people were more welcoming than any of the other tribes he'd known.

Konspewa approved of Chick's skills as a warrior, but he hid concerns that Chick might be part of the Powhatan alliance, or worse, not a chief or important member of his tribe at all. But Konspewa was a man of his word, and if Tesi wished it, he would allow the romance of this man and his daughter.

Tesi did not share her father's concerns and soon decided she would marry this stranger from the eastern shore.

Rabbit

At the giant steel towers of the Sky Ride we pack into an elevator. People crowd the windows, and we pick up speed. Then the elevator jolts to a stop, and we stumble against each other. After we start to move again, we don't stop until we reach a landing half way to the top. Several people get out to board a cabled train of rocket cars that crosses over the lagoon. Mama, Doc, and I continue to the top of the tower. From six hundred feet high you begin to see the curvature of the earth. The windows of the Chicago skyscrapers shimmer with gold light. Doc hands me a dime for the telescope, and I scan the Fair. Dinosaurs pose on buildings. Ant-sized people shuffle in and out of an oriental temple. An eagle on a pedestal stretches her wings. Wildlife like nothing on our farm.

When time expires the telescope blinks off. We watch a little longer from the railing, shading our eyes with our hands. Then we ride the elevator down to the rocket cars. We hold hands as we step into the next car that creeps along. The car in front of us blasts steam into the air, on its way to Mars. Then we lurch forward, and my head smacks against the seat. (At this fair, you have to pay attention.) The lagoon floods the world below us.

—One day, the loud speaker says, we will go to Mars.

I think about that. Mars is a lot farther away than Colorado or Virginia.

That Wednesday, Rosa was standing by the kitchen door when I got to the house after saying goodbye to Billy at the bridge. I set my books on a chair and picked up a freshly baked cracker from a plate on the table. As I skipped back out the door, she didn't ask where I was going, just:

—Be back before dark. Well before dark.

—Yes, ma'am.

I crossed the road and climbed to my lookout.

The woods smelled like rain. I closed my eyes. A raven croaked above me. I practiced my journey. *This is my starting point. From here, I go along the ridge, down the slope along the deer trail, and to the seep. I drink the clear water, and I'm lifted up.*

I heard someone singing. A string of thin notes danced into the sky, the way Rosa sings sometimes. Puffy aster seeds floated by. Then I, too, was floating and suddenly afraid. What was happening? I counted my breaths to calm myself and felt someone's hand lightly touch my arm.

I remembered waking one morning with Charles sitting in the chair beside my bed.

—Get up lazy bones.

I jumped on his back, and we laughed our way to breakfast.

How old was I then? Uncle Charles seemed young but looked the same as now.

Poppy said:

—See what's right in front of you, Eva.

I opened my eyes and saw the hand clasping mine. I looked into her face and tried to speak. But I couldn't. She squeezed my hand and rested her head against the mossy rock. We sat side by side breathing as one until I fell asleep.

Doc and Mama lie on the grass along the bank of the lagoon, hats shading their faces. After a second day at the World's Fair, you need a break. Nearby, other Fair visitors relax or picnic at benches and tables or lounge on the grass. The water reflects the bright sunshine; even the bank sparkles. I pull off my shoes and socks and splash my toes in the little waves along the water's edge. It's colder than Mill Creek in December. That's a problem I see with the north: it's too cold for wading.

A gondola full of laughing people glides near the shore. The standing gondolier waves to me, then returns to his work, propelling the craft forward with his long oar. A woman nearby is reading. I look closer. *A Miscellany of American Poetry 1920.* That's the year Billy was born, a year before me.

Which reminds me … of him, *earlier* in the afternoon that Wednesday. We were walking home, memorizing Edgar Allen Poe's poem, "Annabel Lee."

I walk along the bank, reciting it to myself, again.

It was many and many a year ago,
    In a kingdom by the sea,
That a maiden there lived whom you may know
    By the name of Annabel Lee;—
And this maiden she lived with no other thought
    Than to love and be loved by me.

She was a child and *I* was a child,
    In this kingdom by the sea,
But we loved with a love that was more than love—
    I and my Annabel Lee—
With a love that the wingéd seraphs of Heaven
    Coveted her and me.

And this was the reason that, long ago,
    In this kingdom by the sea,
A wind blew out of a cloud by night
    Chilling my Annabel Lee;
So that her high-born kinsmen came
    And bore her away from me,
To shut her up in a sepulchre
    In this kingdom by the sea.

The angels, not half so happy in Heaven,
      Went envying her and me;
Yes! that was the reason (as all men know,
      In this kingdom by the sea)
That the wind came out of the cloud, chilling
      And killing my Annabel Lee.

But our love it was stronger by far than the love
      Of those who were older than we —
      Of many far wiser than we —
And neither the angels in Heaven above
      Nor the demons down under the sea
Can ever dissever my soul from the soul
      Of the beautiful Annabel Lee: —

For the moon never beams without bringing me dreams
      Of the beautiful Annabel Lee;
And the stars never rise but I see the bright eyes
      Of the beautiful Annabel Lee;
And so, all the night-tide, I lie down by the side
Of my darling, my darling, my life and my bride
      In the sepulchre there by the sea —
      In her tomb by the side of the sea.

I said:

— There are six strophes. Each one has six lines, and the third and the sixth have eight.

— And the fifth strophe has seven lines. So, 6-6-8, 6-7-8.

— Six times six is 36, plus … two, four, five, so 41 lines in all. So we'll need 41 places, one for each line.

Places for things. You can remember anything if you use the method. Places for the lines of a poem. Places for important events in your life. Places for the people you want to remember. Rosa once helped me memorize fifty wild plants we can eat or use for medicine. We created four areas, one for each season. Winter plants were up in the barn and pastures. Spring plants in town.

Summer around the mill and Aunt Katie's. And Fall in the rooms of our house. Within each season area, we designated a place for each plant, where we named the plant and placed images of its useful parts (berry, root, leaf, flower).

—Rhyme scheme, Billy said. It looks like one sound is dominant (sea, Lee, we, me). Sounds like you, *E* va.

—Or Bill-y. It's a common sound.

—I don't think so.

We read from the copies we'd written out in class that day. Miss Powers taught us to remember by writing and reciting lines aloud, over and over. But Poppy says repetition is only one factor when you're committing something to memory. You also have to see the images that represent the words and ideas. And see the images in specific locations along a journey. The journey preserves their order. And it's helpful to look for patterns.

I said:

—The last words of the first strophe … Ago, sea. Know, Lee. Thought, me. AB AB CB. *Thought* doesn't rhyme with any of the others.

—But the next strophe is different. Child, see. Love, Lee. Heaven, me.

—That makes it: AB CB DB. Neither *Child*, *Love*, nor *Heaven* rhyme with each other.

—Right, Billy said, but it gets more interesting. The third strophe, eight lines, is like the second but with one more pair: AB CB DB EB. Sea, Lee, me, sea. Poe sure liked that sound.

—Sure. And the fourth strophe is the same as the second: AB CB DB. And the fifth strophe adds one line. So it's AB *B* CB DB, a six-line strophe plus one *line*, not paired.

—Yes, Billy said, but look: "Of those who were older than we— / Of many far wiser than we—" It's as if he's just emphasizing, saying almost the same thing but associating *older* and *wiser*.

—But older doesn't necessarily mean wiser. Look at the last strophe: AB CB DD BB. Which is nothing like the rest. Rhymes but not straight ones.

—Yes, but really there's only one couplet that's really

different: "Of my darling, my darling, my life and my bride."
Bride is his special ending. I like Poe.

—I like you.

Billy blushed and said hurriedly:

—We'll start with an image for each line, right?

—Yes, but first, let's decide on a journey.

—Of course, this is *our* journey.

He grinned and bumped shoulders with me. Now I blushed.
Then he said:

—How about ...

1. The bus stop where we get off
2. The Fletcher's house
3. Your Aunt Katie's house
4. The edge of the woods above the pastures
5. The path up to the ridge
6. Haunted cabin or whatever it was we saw

—So, I whispered, we'll leave out the still.

—You don't have to whisper. Didn't you hear? The Twenty-
first Amendment, a repeal of the Eighteenth. States are ratifying
the Constitution of the United States. It's never been done before.

—I guess Nathaniel will be glad about that.

—Dad says it's a big deal for everyone, and it might lead to
other changes. California voted to ratify in July, and Virginia's
vote becomes official today.

—Today?

—Yep, Dad read it in the paper this morning.

I watch Doc and Mama on the grass. Doc's sitting up now,
reading a paper. I call to him:

—Do you hear that?

—Is this a game? Doc says.

—Yes, I say, walking up to them. Call it *All the Sounds We
Hear*. Rowing, water lapping.

Doc says:

The shadows of the ships
Rock on the crest
In the low blue lustre
Of the tardy and the soft inrolling tide.

—Who's that?

—Carl Sandburg. He lived in Chicago, but he grew up in a small town west of here, Galesburg. The train goes through it. (*Then he continues the game.*) The Sky Ride motor.

—Mama breathing.

—Voices of people on the gondolas.

—Voices of people on the street.

—Music.

—Yes. That's what I heard, but what's the tinkling sound?

Doc leans over and kisses Mama who opens her eyes.

—We'll be right back, he says. Gotta check out a tinkling sound.

Mama laughs, propping herself on her elbows.

—It's a glass player.

She points along the shore to a small band.

—Do you see the man there? Next to the ... what do you call it? A see-saw, right?

—I see it! Saw it.

—He fills glasses with different amounts of water, or glasses of different sizes, and each makes a different note when he taps them with a spoon.

—How does that work?

—A glass with more empty volume makes a lower pitch, just like when a longer string on the piano gets hit, it makes a lower pitch.

—Is that why men have lower voices?

—Something like that.

I listen to the music of spoon hitting glasses and remember the creek gurgling alongside us that afternoon. Goosebumps run down my arms.

Doc says:

—I hate to spoil this mood, but we've got to get back to the train soon. We'll be heading west in an hour.

—Southwest, I say. Southwest on the *Chief*.

Late afternoon, I've come to the observation car to write. I barely notice when the train pulls out of Union Station. Each time I look up, another building disappears behind us. Then we start across a bridge, another river below us.

—Which one is this?

—The Fox, Doc says.

—Look (*Mama points*), we're on an island now.

—I didn't know rivers had islands.

—If they're big enough, Doc says, like the James back home, around Lynchburg. Didn't you listen to Poppy's story?

The island looks like a park, with tall trees and smooth grass. I wonder if there are foxes on the island. Or rabbits. Do islands have animals? Of course they do, Billy would say. But how do they get there?

The sun and the horizon are starting to eye each other, to tempt each other, and we're surrounded by farmland. Two snow white bunnies race across a plowed field of black soil. Farther on I see two horses, one black one white, running together, their long manes and tails flowing behind them. Then I see our farm, Sargent in the pasture, Poppy leading him to the barn.

But it's an hour later there, already dark. Sargent is in his stall by now. Poppy is already in the kitchen with Rosa, washing up for supper. Doc says the time zones came about because of train travel. We all needed to be on time or we'd miss the train. Before time zones, travelers could easily become confused. But if you stayed home, it didn't matter.

Meanwhile at Chick's home along the Chickahominy, Wink tried to explain Chick's unusual behavior to the older, wise ones in the group who were disturbed by his long absence.

—Give him until harvest, Wink tried to reassure them. And if he has not returned, we'll consider our options.

—We must find a replacement, to lead us in our visions, they insisted.

Wink sent word to Chick that Opech's alliance, which Chick's people had reluctantly become a part of, had suffered tremendous losses in a battle with the golden ones, a massacre that would forever be remembered. The golden ones grew in power and took life as if it were not life at all. Wink suggested that Opech's forces might be weaker when Chick returned, but in his heart, Wink believed the golden ones had become the more serious threat.

Wink's message reached Chick four and a half years after Chick left home. Chick had been married two years to Tesi, and they were expecting a child soon. Chick was conflicted but knew he must return and assist loyal Wink. When Chick explained the letter to Konspewa and Tesi, Konspewa offered a full escort to return home with him, and much to Konspewa's sorrow and Chick's concern, Tesi insisted on going with them. Father and husband tried to convince her to wait until the child was born, but she refused to live without Chick. As they loaded the canoes, they hoped and prayed that Tesi's time would not come before they reached the Chickahominy.

The River

We have ten minutes before our turn for supper. Mama gets up to return her book, *The Art of Fugue*, to our sleeping compartment. She says that even if you can't play music you can still think about it. I read the guidebook that Doc gave me as we were leaving the station in Chicago. We're approaching Galesburg, where Carl Sandburg grew up and where Abraham Lincoln debated Stephen Douglas in 1858. Miss Powers told us about that. Illinois was a prominent anti-slavery state, and the first anti-slavery society in Illinois was started in Galesburg. It was also part of the Underground Railroad.

—Those were hard times, Miss Powers said, if you were a person of color in the United States.

I think about that and the time Billy taught me Hangman. It was raining that day, too hard for Miss Powers to send us outdoors for recess. Miss Powers loves to keep us working on rainy days. That Thursday, no matter what she had us do, we were glad to be inside. No one argued. The storm was a frog strangler; we could hear it pounding the playground, so loudly that we almost had to shout to be heard. Miss Powers finally gave up; she stared out the window and watched it pour.

—I can't believe you've never played Hangman, Billy said.

We pushed our desks together near a window.

—Sure as day, I've never heard of Hangman.

—It's simple. One of us picks a word and writes a dash for each letter. Above that, you draw a scaffold. The other person guesses letters that might be in the word. If she guesses right, he writes the letter where it belongs. If the letter isn't in the word, then a body part goes up on the scaffold. If your entire body goes up before the word is solved, you're a hanged man.

—Or woman! How do you know when to stop adding body parts?

—You decide ahead of time. Head, torso, two arms, and two legs. That's where we'll start.

He drew in his notebook: a simple scaffold and below it, seven dashes, a space, and five more dashes.

—Two words? I asked.

He smiled.

Seven, five … I thought about that and came up with:

—It could be general store. Or chamber music. Or Maurice Ravel. Or Potomac River …

—Or cynthia moths, he shot back. Or country music? Hermann Hesse? Come on, what's your letter guess?

—General: G-e-n-e-r-a-l. Seven letters. How about a G?

—Nope, there's your head.

Billy drew a circle under the scaffold, and I guessed again.

—E.

That one worked. He put an E at the sixth location: _ _ _ _ _ E _   _ _ _ _ _

—How about A?

—Yep. _ A _ _ _ E _   _ A _ _ _

—OK, I'll risk another vowel: I

—You lucked out there. _ A _ _ _ E _   _ A _ I _

—L?

—Torso.

—M?

—Arm.

—OK, wait. Let me think.

—Might as well. Looks like you'll be hanging soon.

I thought a moment, then said:

—N?

—Hmm. Eva, that's a bit too lucky. Are you cheating? _ A _ _ _ E _   _ A _ I N

—Of course I'm not cheating. How could I? I'm just being logical. First vowels, then consonants. I shouldn't have wasted that G earlier. How about T?

He grimaced. _ A _ _ T E _ _ A _ I N

Then I guessed H, and from there it was easy, nothing for Billy to do except admit I wasn't hanged yet.

We're finishing supper (mashed potatoes, bread with butter, baked beans, and collard greens) when Doc says:

—We'll reach the Mississippi soon.

—Can I go to the observation car?

—You could. But how would you like to see the river from the end of the train?

—The caboose?

—More or less. Follow me. Leah, do you want to come?

—No, you two go. I want to finish my coffee, and I'm content to watch from the observation car.

We reach the last car and step outside. Standing at the rail in the cool evening air, we look back toward where we're coming from. Nestled between tangled dark tree trunks, the tracks glide away from us. Or seem to. Tracks don't move.

We catch ourselves as we shift to the right when the train turns, slowing for the bridge that I know must be coming. We start across, and there it is below our feet, the Mississippi River. As we cross it grows wider, and the trees on the shore disappear into twilight. The water glows orange in the setting sunlight, the light of the sun I know must be behind me now, leading our train forward, westward.

But our view grows narrower as the bridge draws around us.

—Why is it so closed in? I ask.

—Double-decker, the cars cross above us.

The conductor calls back down the aisle:

—Santa Fe Swing Bridge, just six years new, folks. Double-deck, swing-span, longest of its kind.

It's loud as the clanking of our car reverberates off the metal bridge, and automobiles I imagine rumble above us.

—The Santa Fe? I say.

—For the Santa Fe rail line.

—And we'll be in Santa Fe …

—Tomorrow afternoon.

The bars and rails clutter around us in a kaleidoscope of geometric designs. Then the tracks grow quieter again, and I can see the bridge we've just crossed. And we turn again, slowly still, passing through another town.

—What are those? I ask.

—Warehouses, factories. Hard to say.

—Not many windows.

—That's the way it is with manufacturing. Walls are cheaper than windows.

Some of the small ones look like houses. Next to one, children play ball in a dirt lot.

—Are those people poor?

—Yes, but it's not their fault. Their parents can't find work.

—Don't they want to work?

—Most of them do. But sometimes just wanting to work isn't enough.

—Like *Mrs. Wiggs and the Cabbage Patch.*

—Yes, like that.

The last thing I see clearly is the house with the children. They seem to be looking at me. I remember Poppy and the rivers back home. I remember looking down at Aunt Katie's house getting smaller and smaller as Billy and I climbed, searching for the haunted cabin.

As we walk back toward the observation car, I say:

—I want to see every river crossing between here and Colorado.

—Sure. But you might have to stay up late for that.

—Will Mama mind?

—I don't think so.

Tesi's contractions began as they canoed through the jagged cut in the Blue Ridge that separates the high mountain valleys from the flat eastern country. The sky darkened with cumulus. Then rain and hail pummeled the creeks, and the river rose. Chick and his men in the leading canoe tried to get ashore, but the swift current hurled them farther downriver. In one of the last canoes, Mayengieqta, Tesi's nurse, tried to slow the contractions. She wrapped her garments and body around Tesi as she had when Tesi was born. True to Mayengieqta's name which meant "a bird's nest" she sheltered them, one within the other. Mayen cooed softly, trying to imprint her slow deep breaths upon Tesi's. But even a bird's nest is vulnerable to ravaging storms, and every jolt in the river urged the baby onward, outward. Everything was happening too quickly, and Tesi delivered mid-river, the storm smothering her cries.

Much later, they found a place to land the canoes, and Chick felt miraculously saved. But his rejoicing was short-lived. Mayen held out the softly breathing babe.

—Hold your child, she said, her face thick with tears. She is all you have left of your beautiful queen.

Chick gathered the baby girl in his arms and wept.

When he recovered enough to speak, he said to his infant daughter:

—Of all the great gifts and blessings that will come to you in this world, none will be able to replace your loss this day as you entered the world. Marina, I will call you, for the currents in this river were like the mighty waves upon the endless sea that I'd hoped to show your mother, my queen.

The men tried to console Chick, but they finally interrupted his grieving to say they must get back on the river soon and leave Tesi's body. The water spirits were angry, and a dead body, even a queen's, onboard would only provoke them further.

—We'll not send her down the river! Chick said with fear in his eyes. And her body will not be safe here on this saturated shore. Wild animals and birds will find her.

But the others persisted, fearing their priest was falling from them and that they must do whatever they could to appease the spirits. When Chick finally relented, he silently took the smallest canoe up the bank. He bedded it with greenery and placed Tesi within. His men helped him find fine smooth stones, which he placed around her. Softly, Chick said to his men:

— Let me be.

They left him to finish his mourning in solitude. Alone now, Chick placed a single red maple leaf on her bosom and onto it, pressed a smooth, flat dark brown stone. Around the stone, he arranged twenty pieces of amber, one for each year of her life, and representing the petals of her secret spirit flower, the deer eye.

Chick said a prayer and removed his deerskin robe. He spread it out on a soft patch of ground. From his pouch he extracted his sacred rattlesnake tooth and with the fang etched the story of his love on the deerskin. He rolled the deep charcoal colored humus in his hands and pressed the soil into the lines of the images. When the earth had dried on the skin, he wrapped the robe about his wife.

The images on the robe lay against her skin, facing her, so that she and the Great Spirit would know who she was. So that she could walk the Path of Souls in this robe and treasure her memories while moving onto the next world. As she walked the Path, the great river of stars, she would go in knowledge and be free to move to the Otherworld. Her secret names would stay wrapped safely against her body so that no man on earth would know to utter them, and therefore she would not be tempted to linger within the physical world.

Chick knelt beside the canoe and imagined their futures. He saw her riding calmly over smooth waters. He saw himself looking up at the wide river of stars. He felt her spirit walking the Path, and he knew they were ready.

Chick called to two of his companions, who helped him make a lid for the canoe. They tied it shut, braced it on their shoulders, and started hiking into the mountains. After they had walked for several hours, they found a calm stream. At its bank, Chick lit a bundle of sweetgrass and, sending the aromatic smoke in the seven directions, chanted softly while his companions eased the coffin canoe into the water.

—May the spirits shield her and love her, Chick said.

After his companions had started down the trail, Chick turned once more to the canoe gliding out of sight.

—Wait for me, in the womb of our Mother Earth.

By the time they returned to their canoes the storm had subsided; the water spirits had been appeased. But the baby needed milk; Mayen's was insufficient. So they changed course and started poling back to Two Rivers.

—See it, Eva? Doc says.

—What? Where?

—The window, hurry. It's the Des Moines.

I just see the edge of the water. The sky is all violet and salmon colored. I can see the reflection in the water.

—So soon after the Mississippi?

—It's got a lot of tributaries.

That reminds me of Mill Creek again, turning to run into the South, the Maury, the James.

The Sacred River, that's what Poppy calls it.

—Picture this, Eva.

Poppy and Eva had left the house at sunset. The ground was spongy, and the grasses bent from the drenching rain earlier that day. Eva stopped to gaze at the moon.

—Exactly half, she said.

—Ah, yes. Halfway between empty and full, new and old.

(*He took her hand.*) Birth and death, this world and the next.

   — Is that part of the tradition?

   — It is.

   — How will we find our way back in the dark?

   — By the light of the moon of course.

They continued walking from the ridge down to the river. And Eva said:

   — Do you hear that?

   — They've started singing.

   — Who are they?

The music reminded Eva of Charles playing long still notes on his pan pipes. Their voices were like reeds blowing in the wind.

A woman, in a dark blue almost black dress, appeared from the mist and stood at the bank.

She was tall and older, kissing Poppy's forehead. She bent to kiss me, and her earrings and abalone necklace sparkled in the moonlight. She smelled of jasmine, primrose, night-blooming flowers. Her strong hands held my head to her chest for a long time.

She led me to a shallow pool. Three women waited, knee deep in the water, their red, blue, and green dresses floating around them. Their eyes shown blue, and their hair was the lightest blond I'd ever seen.

The older woman nodded to Poppy, who took a bundle of peach and yellow leaves from a basket and tossed them into the pool. She motioned for me to sit on a smooth rock where she removed my shoes. She encircled my neck with a strand of purple beads and raven feathers.

As she guided me into the water, my dress floated like a pond lily. As she backed away, the other women took my hands and began singing. The reflection of the moon floated on the water

with the leaves. I felt warmth spreading through me. My hands,
my arms. I closed my eyes and pushed my toes into the mud. My
entire body felt warm and wet. I inhaled. Was this heaven?

Then I must have fallen asleep. I was on the porch swing
cradled in Poppy's lap, wrapped in his coat. I knew I'd just been
with my great-grandmother, Iris.

In my dream—

we take a familiar path
to the ridge
down the other side

to the seep
where Poppy stops
to drink

I tap the water
with my hand
and make that splat splat

sound that echoes
someone comes
to sit beside me

a young girl
takes my hand
I try to speak

I can barely breathe.

I see a woman in a dark gown standing beside us. Black
feathers dangle from her ears. I recognize her. She picks up the

girl and hands her to a man who has appeared nearby. I cry, I don't know why, as the woman bends down and puts her forehead to mine.

—In time, she says, you will understand, my love.

Wolf

I must have dozed. Doc is patting my shoulder.
　— What?
　— Don't you want to see the Missouri River?
　— Where?
　— There.

I look out the window and see the dark swath of water. We're across it before I'm completely awake. Doc says:

— Some people call it the Big Muddy. We'll be alongside it for a while. Why don't you get some sleep, and I'll wake you when we stop in Kansas City.

He guides me to our compartment and turns on a lamp.

— I think I'll write in my journal.

— Of course. You can always sleep later.

He winks. I kiss him goodnight, change into my pajamas, crawl into bed, and write.

At the farm Mama was playing a song that started low and slow. Then it rose and exploded into high air, before falling into dreamlike sadness.

— What is it? I said when she stopped to work though a section again. It's so complicated, almost twisted.

She nodded.

— Hugo Wolf, the man who wrote it, suffered from mental turmoil. And a disease, syphilis, worsened his mood swings. I was only five when he died in Vienna, but I remember because my piano teacher, who was an emotional woman, was in tears that day. But I find a kind of peace in his music. He was inspired by poetry. This song is set to Goethe's "*Kennst du das land?*"

—Something … the land?

—Do you know the land. It's a poem about a land of lemon blossoms and golden oranges … Come stand behind me.

She took my hands and covered her eyes with them and then started playing. She calls this her *muscle memory* exercise. Doc thinks it's like what the dancer Martha Graham calls *blood memory*, which I think means you're digging into the deep roots of your ancestry to express ideas.

When she finished, she pulled my arms around her neck and kissed my hands.

—I don't know, I said. I still think it's awfully sad.

—Maybe I'm not playing it quite right. It's supposed to be impassioned but with more yearning than sadness. It's about a girl who remembers her home in Italy after being forced …

She stopped, then looked down at the keys and repeated a section with her right hand several times.

—Mama. Forced to what?

—Eva. (*She brought her hand back to the bench, her shoulders tense.*) Forced to sing and dance and … in a new place. She was forced to live in a place far from her home.

No. I shook my head and stepped back. *So she knew how terrible it was going to be. She knew it deep in her blood. Then why was she letting it happen?*

—But the piece is hopeful, she said. She's telling her protector that it is possible to return home. It's the yearning, the desire, which makes seeming impossibilities possible.

No. I felt tears coming and turned away. *Was she trying to enact the song? Trying to show me what she went through leaving* her *home? Why?*

—I know it's hard, Eva. It's hard for all of us.

—Then why? I almost shouted.

She drew my hands back into hers and kissed them again.

—It's a long story, and I can't explain it all now. Trust us. If there were another solution, we'd take it.

—But *why?*

She looked down at the keys, then said:

—Why don't you ... Why don't you go play with Kleela. She'll cheer you up.

That's when *it* hit me.

—Is Kleela coming with us? I said.

—Darling ...

I ran from the room, hot with tears.

—Kleela, I called.

We ran down to the road, across the field, and toward the lookout. I didn't look back.

When we got to the rocks I was breathing too hard to cry anymore, and I felt defeated. *How can they do this to me? To us? Our family? What could have gone so wrong that led to this?* I cupped my head in my hands.

When I heard Kleela growl, I looked up. Her hair stood on the back of her neck. I turned in the direction she was looking, back down to the farm. A black car had stopped just before the bridge, and Charles came out of the mill, walking toward the car. Of course, I was too far away to hear anything. But I think Kleela did. She growled under her breath. As Charles got closer to the car, it looked like a man said something, his arm reaching from the window. And then the car suddenly backed up, spun around, and sped down the road.

I was still watching when *she* tapped my shoulder, singing softly:

E-o-ah.

I turned and saw her, beautiful strands of red and white beads around her neck. I remembered the water ceremony. She smiled and sat next to me, light as a feather.

—Ave? I said.

She took my hand.

—I'm ... I'm Eva. You're Ave?

She smiled, turned, and pointed back toward the Blue Ridge. Then she touched her eyes and pointed again.

—You sleep in the mountains?

She nodded and touched her eyes again, pointing toward the mountains.

—Look in the mountains? You see things in the mountains?

She nodded.

— What do you see?

She touched her eyes, then my chest with her long finger.

— You see me? Or I see? What do I see? Who are you?

She pointed again toward the mountains, then toward the farm, and she stepped her hands down, slowly, leaning forward. But the sun caught her eye, and she flinched, leaping from the rock. She took a few steps into the woods and motioned for me to follow.

I slipped down from the rock and followed her along the ridge as the farm went in and out of view. She walked deliberately, each step silent. I tried to imitate her, but the leaves still crunched beneath me.

If she was following a path, I didn't see it. I looked for landmarks: a stump, a steep drop on one side, a dogwood. When the farm had been out of sight too long I stopped.

But Ave kept going, following Kleela now through a thicker woods of white oaks I didn't recognize. I wasn't sure what to do, but I told myself Kleela would find our way back even if I couldn't.

We passed a seep gurgling out of the rocks, and she looked back at me and smiled, then hopped across the trickle.

We came out to a river, a sandy beach, and pools that felt familiar. Ave turned and gently touched my face. Then she pointed to her eyes, then past the river, into the dark woods on the other side.

I saw a woman standing in the water. Her arms stretched toward me, but she seemed to be looking past me. I knew someone was behind me, and I sensed this wasn't happening now, but at some other time. Charles stepped past me and into the water. He held a bundle in his arms and handed it to the woman. When he stepped back, I saw the child.

Chick returned to Two Rivers
where Manki and Mihani pledged
to raise Marina as if she were
their own daughter.

For they too had been blessed
with a daughter two moons earlier.
Chick left Marina
in his friends' loyal care.

His heart was heavy, buoyed only
by hope that he would return soon
to his red bird babe,
that love would right itself.

After listening to Poppy's story, Eva went to the study where Doc and Leah were talking.
— Mama, Doc?
— Come in, Doc said.
— Sometimes, Eva began slowly. Sometimes we have to leave things behind, just for a little while, until things work out.
— That's right, Doc said. Like leaving Poppy and the farm. We'll see them again.
— I know, but ... I think there's a better way. You could leave me with Poppy and Grandma Rosa. I can help on the farm, and school's just—
— Eva, Doc interrupted.
Then Leah said softly:
— Doc.
Doc said:
— That is entirely out of the question. I am very sorry. I know

this is not your ideal scenario.

—Wait! You didn't let me finish. Not for forever, just till the end of the —

—Eva. I don't want to hear any more. We're not going to change our plans. This is for the best. You need to trust us.

—But I don't understand how you can do this to me. Did you ever ask me what I thought? How I'd feel? About leaving Poppy and the farm and … Just listen to me. (*Tears wet her red cheeks.*) I found someone. I …

—Eva, this is hard for all of us.

—Just … just until the end of the school year.

—Young lady, Doc said firmly, this is the end of the discussion.

—But you always said it doesn't hurt—

—Eva May.

—You said it doesn't hurt to dream.

Eva ran from the study and up to her room, slamming the door behind her.

When I stopped crying, I could hear Doc and Mama talking. Doc said:

—It'll be over soon. I thought we agreed she could enjoy these last days, that it'd be safer this way. Charles said *he* came by again. We can't hold him off much longer.

Then Mama said something in German and started crying.

I was so confused and angry. Why wasn't I being told anything? Who was *he*? Who couldn't be held off any longer? The only one who wanted to tell me anything was Ave. And as far as I could tell, she couldn't speak. Even Poppy. Why would he keep things from me? I wanted to be Marina. Mama and Doc could go away if they wanted to.

I heard the porch door slam. What was happening? I tiptoed into the hallway.

That's when I got the idea. I went back into my room, pulled on my thick sweater, picked up my shoes, and turned on the lamp by my bed. I closed the door quietly, crept down the stairs, and went outside. I walked deliberately, toes first on the ground, heels up, the way Ave walked.

I slipped behind the tulip poplar and put my shoes on. Then I ran across the road. Kleela followed.

—Go back, I told her.

But she wouldn't.

—Kleela, I said and nestled my head into hers.

Then I said sternly:

—Stay.

A light shone from the mill, but I didn't see anyone on the porch. So I took my chance and ran. The moon was bright enough for me to get to my lookout. I waited, hoping Ave would know I was there and appear. But it was quiet. Even the crickets were silent.

If light bothers her (I remembered her flinching at the sun) then she should like the night.

The lights from the farm flickered and seemed far way. I didn't care about staying in sight. I started along the ridge, the direction I'd gone with Ave. Soon I was on the other side, but I couldn't tell exactly where I was. I thought I was going through the oaks, but they looked different. I expected to come to the seep. A few minutes later, I knew I was on the wrong track. I turned and climbed back to the ridge. But I was somewhere else; the farm wasn't below me. And the moon had set.

I heard something. A motor? My stomach felt queasy. I started walking in the direction I hoped would lead home. I tripped and fell to my hands. As I pushed myself up, I thought of snakes. I heard that creaking sound I'd heard with Billy. It was coming from where I was headed. Something was coming toward me. I wanted to run, but where? It was an animal. There was nothing but darkness. I cried out.

—Kleela.

I was so relieved; I held her to me.

—I love you. Take us home.

101

She turned, and I followed her away from the frightening noises.

When we got back in sight of the farm, I saw tail lights. And the light at the mill was still on; so was our kitchen light. I crept through the back door.

In my room, I scolded myself for being so foolish. I was lucky I hadn't been caught. I buried my face in my pillow. I could have gotten really lost. But that train of thought stopped as I heard Rosa say:

—Everything has a purpose.

Raccoon

We reach the outskirts of another city, lights sparkling in an otherwise dark landscape. I get out of bed, pull on my robe, and walk to the observation car. Doc's there reading a thick blue book he bought at a bookstore in Chicago, *An Experiment With Time*.

—Hi, honey. I thought you were sleeping.

—No. Writing.

—Good, good.

—Where are we?

—Almost in Kansas City.

—How's your book?

—Excellent. Dunne's got an interesting idea.

—About?

—About how dreams work. He thinks we can dream the future. He and Poppy would enjoy talking with each other.

I look out the window. White buildings stand out from the darkness around them.

—Can I stay up with you and write?

—Sure, get your things.

It was early Saturday morning, and I had climbed to the lookout after breakfast. Billy was coming over around ten so we could plan our Halloween masks and finish memorizing "Annabel Lee." I had hoped to find Ave before he arrived.

She was there, waiting. She hugged me, took my hand, and motioned for me to sit beside her.

I pointed to the farm.

—That's where I live.

Ave nodded and pointed toward the farm.

—Do you want to go?

No, she shook her head. With her right hand, she tapped behind her left shoulder, then her chest, and then she waved her hand low and pointed toward the farm. She repeated the motions: back, chest, low, farm.

—Back when you were little?

She nodded.

—Do you go to school?

She wiggled her hand back and forth as if to say *sort of, not really.*

—Where do you live?

She pointed back to the mountains. Then she took my hand and with it, she gently patted my chest and held it there. With her other hand, she patted her chest. Then she released my hand and brought her hands together in a silent clap.

—We're together?

She nodded.

—Ave, may I call you Ave?

She nodded.

—I'm leaving soon. I have to go far away.

She nodded.

—I mean for a long time. I don't know when I'll be back.

She nodded, then pointed to me and stretched her arms wide.

—Do you know everything?

She smiled and closed her eyes. So I did too. And I imagined I was walking along the river. A woman with long silver hair stretched her arms and accepted a child. But the child in her arms was me! How could that be? I looked at the woman's face and tried to speak.

—*Ice, Ice,* I said.

She twinkled one hand in front of me and kissed my cheek. Then I knew it wasn't me. I was watching. I heard footsteps. I reached for Ave beside me but felt only air. Then:

—Gotcha, Billy said.

—Billy Morgan, I said, standing. You … Billy, you …

—What, I scare you?

He was looking up at me from the base of the rocks. I realized my hands were on my hips just like Mama, so I released them and said:

—But … Didn't you see me talk—

No. He'd think I was crazy.

—Of course I heard you, and I was wondering who you were talking to. But I didn't mean to scare you.

—You didn't.

—Good. Who were you talking to? Were you working on "Annabel Lee"?

—No. Well, not really. I heard your footsteps. It's just that … (*I thought a moment*) I was doing a memory journey, not our poem, just … another one.

He climbed up and sat where Ave had just been. He reached for my hand.

—Come on, he said, pulling me back down. Poppy told me you were here.

—He did? How did he know? Oh, never mind.

We sat quietly until I knew I had to say something.

—You wanna hear something crazy?

—Sure, he said.

—Please don't laugh.

—I won't. What is it?

—Promise?

—Cross my heart and hope to die.

I took a deep breath and looked into his blue eyes.

—I found a girl up here. I don't know who she is. She's about our age, but she doesn't go to school, or at least not to our school. I call her Ave, but … I don't think she can talk. She just motions.

—Go on.

—She has pale skin. Her fingers are long and thin. And (*I took another deep breath*) I think I've seen her, or someone a lot like her, in my dreams, since I was little. Then one day not long ago

I saw her. For real. When I hear the hermit thrush in the woods, I think she's calling my name. And it's almost as if she's a spirit: she's here, then gone.

—You mean she disappears into thin air?

I knew it sounded impossible. Even Billy would think I'd gone round the bend. But he said:

—I've heard of things like that.

—You have?

—OK, you see her, and then she's gone, right? Does anyone else see her?

—Did you?

—Me? When?

—Just now. She was right here. Where you're sitting. I think you scared her.

He shrugged.

—I was probably too far off.

—I know it sounds crazy, but I don't see how she can only be in my imagination. She seems so real. She held my hand. I felt her. You can't feel a spirit can you?

Billy rested his elbows on his knees.

—You see her, and then she's gone?

I nodded.

—And you think you've seen her before?

I nodded.

—But she doesn't talk to you.

—Except …

—Except when a thrush calls, it's like she's calling to you?

I nodded, starting to feel relieved. He was taking me seriously.

—And she's pale, almost like a ghost?

—Her skin is pale. But it's not as though I can see through her, but … Well, I guess I'm not sure what a ghost looks like.

Billy's eyes squinted into the distance. After a little while he said:

—OK. Let's say we have three possibilities. One: she's real, a girl who lives up here in the mountains, in a family we don't know about. Two: she's imaginary, and you've created her through years of thinking about her, or dreaming about her. Or three: she's a spirit, a ghost, maybe someone that died up here.

—OK ... Sure.

—Let's take the first possibility. Have you ever heard of people living up here? In the mountains beyond the river? These woods are dense, remote. It would be easy enough to hide from other people if a family wanted to. Maybe they owe people money. Maybe the dad has been out of work for a long time.

—I've always been told these mountains are too deep and dark to live in. But ... (*I remembered the water ceremony*) maybe she's a runaway? Maybe from the high holler where Grandma Rosa's family is from?

—All right. So it's possible, if not probable. How does she get away so quickly? She distracts you and then disappears. Maybe she's part Indian. They say Indians are good at that. Except you said she's pale, right?

—Yeah. But what if she's just in my mind? Can your mind create something that feels that real?

—Dad says people do. They hallucinate and see things that other people don't see. But ... you don't really want to go there. Some people think seeing stuff that isn't here means you're sick and not fit for society. Dad says they're building a new hospital for people like that. He says they just want to lock up anyone who's different.

My heart raced. It was becoming hard to breathe.

—Don't worry, Billy said. Even if you do see things, Dad says that can be OK too. He says imagination is powerful, something we should cultivate, not be ashamed of. Your Poppy'd say that too, just in different words.

—There's another thing.

—What?

—The other night ... Poppy told me about a water ceremony. It's tradition, something you do in the fall. You know his story; his mother had Indian blood ... Anyhow, it's like a baptism, but in a pool of water in the woods, in a stream. I didn't tell you about it because I fell asleep while he was explaining it, and it's hard to separate what was real from what was a dream. But I'm sure I saw, or dreamt—unless he was just telling me this—an old woman down by the river. It's a woman I keep seeing in my … There's something else. I've been having dreams where I seem to be observing the dream as much as being in it. I can't even be sure the ceremony was real. Wherever I was, there were people at the river. Three women. And one of them was …

I stopped. I had to rethink everything. What had I seen exactly? Billy waited silently, looking at me as if he had all the time in the world.

I continued:

—Earlier today when I was with Ave, I saw the woman again, down by the river. In my mind, I mean. And I had this feeling I knew her, that she might be my great-grandmother Iris, Poppy's mother.

—Wow, Billy said. Maybe you are seeing a ghost!

—Why do you think it's a ghost?

—Remember what your Grandma Rosa said about the veil?

—This time of year the veil between the worlds gets thin.

—Maybe the girl's from a different time.

Billy was getting excited.

—I guess she'd have to be from the past if she were a ghost.

—Or maybe the future? Billy said, grinning. Who knows where ghosts come from.

—What?

—Yes, and maybe that explains why she looks different. So let's say that ghosts are possible—that we can see people after they're dead. Maybe the old woman was an Indian that died up here, and that's why she looks different. Or maybe she's the grandmother of the girl spirit you keep seeing.

—She did have feathers and make-up, or face paint. I guess that could make her an Indian.

—And the girl?

—She's pale, but that would be right if she's a ghost. And Poppy says if you go way back there was a race of fair-skinned people in these mountains. Maybe she's an old ghost of the moon people.

Billy thought about that, then said:

—Can you touch a ghost?

—Doesn't seem right. But I've held her hand.

—I guess that part could be your imagination?

—Where does all this get us? I sighed. We're just guessing.

—It must be important to you.

—I thought you'd think I was crazy.

—I do. That's why I like you.

He leaned toward me and kissed my cheek. I turned. *Billy Morgan*. And before I could think another thought, he kissed me on the lips, then hurriedly stood and pulled me up with him.

—Let's go memorize our poem, he said.

We held hands most of the way down the hill. I knew that was real.

—Eva, Billy said, lowering his voice.

We were coming back from the barn where we had been remembering "Annabel Lee" by placing an image for each line at a location along our memory journey.

He said:

—You know this poem is terribly sad. Her kinsmen came and bore her away.

—Yes, I said, looking at him. And I'm sure she didn't want to go.

—Promise you'll write me.

—Will I? You know I will. And you'd better write back.

—Hey, I'm a writer.

Then suddenly all I could think about was his kiss, and I knew I was blushing.

He called as he ran down the road.

—Bye, Eva.

High in the Blue Ridge a clever people practiced an ancient magic. Few people had seen them or even knew they existed. When they were seen, they were usually mistaken for ghosts or phantoms. Their skin glowed like the moon. They lived in a complex labyrinth of caverns within the mountains.

An elder of the people, Cerimon, was renowned as a healer, chemist, and musician. Like that brilliant Greek, Pythagoras, Cerimon's ancestors had known that music, knowledge of nature, and health were interwoven. Like his ancestors, Cerimon observed, studied, and experimented. The walls and tables of his chamber, deep in a cavern, held precious stones, feathers, and other talismans that he had carefully selected during many years of practice. In his underground gardens, strange climbing plants grew without sunlight. A stone table held his instruments: mortar, pestle, jars, bowls, sharp blades, flint, fire, vials of oils. Another table contained scrolls, manuscripts, and writings on skins, stones, all rarities at that time in the Blue Ridge. When asked, he replied that written knowledge contained much of his people's magic, and the writings were gifts from the ancestors.

One day, three of Cerimon's apprentices rushed into his chamber to report a strange canoe they had found while collecting healing clays along the river. Cerimon followed them to the canoe, lodged in the shadowy entrance to the cavern. He removed a burgundy stone from a pouch he always kept with him. When he held the stone before him, a stream of light swam across the canoe. He considered the patterns created by the light. When he saw the signs were good, he handed the stone to one of his apprentices and untied the ropes. Inside the canoe they found the motionless face of a beautiful woman wrapped in a deerskin robe.

—Who are you? Cerimon whispered. Truly a great treasure. But who has sent off such a noble body to travel alone? From where has she come?

His fingers brushed her soft cheeks.

—She was beautiful, he said. She is still. Her face holds blood. She cannot be long …

Realizing the strangeness of her faintly warm flesh, he suddenly turned to his apprentices.

—Quickly, help me carry her. And fetch your flutes. Perhaps they have said goodbye too hastily. Music, heat.

He continued giving orders as they carried her into his chamber.

—Start a fire in the prayer room and bring in hot rocks to surround her. And make sure that nothing prevents the sound of the water from entering the chamber. We must calm her spirit if she decides to return to us.

Cerimon ground herbs together and moistened them with the freshly harvested clays. The apprentices returned with hot rocks. When Cerimon hurriedly pulled aside her coverings, a small white object slipped from the folds and caught his eye. He immediately recognized the shaman's rattlesnake tooth.

—Yes, he said to himself, lifting it up.

He smoothly ran the tooth over her chest and rubbed the poultice into her flesh. Then he selected three vials. He rubbed the oils into her hands, arms, and head while an apprentice massaged her feet and legs. The other two apprentices played flutes and kept the room warm. They worked over her for hours. Cerimon caressed her temples with a special nut oil that came from the heart of the mountains. He spoke quietly, leaning toward her. When he finally straightened, releasing her head, her eyes blinked, and her chest lifted.

She was awake.

Rattlesnake Tooth

An hour later my eyelids are heavy, but I'm still awake as we continue alongside the Kansas River. I can tell from the darkness that we're leaving the cities behind. The land rolls away in simple shadowy strokes.

Doc and Mama sit across from me and don't seem to mind that I haven't gone to bed. They're absorbed in their reading. Mama's book is one she bought in Chicago, *Agriculture of the Hidatsa Indians*.

—How's your book? I ask.

—Mmm, (*her eyes glitter when she looks up*) fascinating. It's about farming practices among the Indian tribes, especially the Hidatsa in North Dakota. Mostly it's told from the point of view of one person: Buffalo Bird Woman.

I try to picture a woman buffalo with wings, but a buffalo is so heavy ... Mama says:

—A researcher from the University of Minnesota spent a few summers with her (*she flips to the front of the book*) 20 years ago, learning her tribe's farming methods. His interviews with her became his Ph.D. thesis and then this book. She died last year.

—Oh. That's too bad, about her dying, I mean. And the book is about her garden?

—Yes. In fact, a better name for the book might be *Buffalo Bird Woman's Garden*.

I flash to Aunt Sadie's garden. She keeps two types of corn on either side of the path that leads up to her house. And when we were there, they were so tangled with squash and beans we could barely see the ears.

—Eva? Doc says. Time for bed?

—I guess so. I was just remembering when you and I went to see Aunt Sadie and Lamont.

—Can you remember from your bed?

Doc leads me back to our sleeping compartment, his hand on my shoulder, moving me onward and steadying me when the train jiggles. I'm so sleepy I'm giddy. It's like waiting up for New Years Eve. I struggle out of my robe (my arms aren't working the way they're supposed to) and climb into the upper berth. I sigh when my head hits the pillow. I giggle when Doc kisses my nose. I turn and bury my face in the soft pillow.

But I'm still remembering …

It was the day Doc and I went to see Aunt Sadie and Lamont, her retarded son. But I probably shouldn't call him retarded. She was standing in the doorway when we came down the path between the rows of corn. When we climbed the steps to the porch, she dusted off her hands on her apron and hugged me. She smelled of flour and something sweet I didn't recognize. She asked us to come in, but Doc said we'd be content sitting on the back porch, which was shaded. So we walked around back, and I sat on a chair and Doc on the swing. Aunt Sadie went back inside and returned with Lamont, who was drooling a little. She sat him down on a rocking chair beside me. After she wiped his mouth with her handkerchief she joined Doc on the swing. We were all settled in and could look into the woods if we had a mind to. But Lamont set his eyes directly on me. So I tried to be polite and returned his look with a smile.

I know it sounds strange, but Lamont looked older than Aunt Sadie, who looked much older than Doc. I asked Doc about that later, and he said it stemmed from Lamont's developmental condition. But he didn't elaborate. Lamont's hair was so short you'd have thought Aunt Sadie must have shaved his head when she cut his hair. His ears stuck out like bat wings. He heard well too, so the short hair-big ear combination had its usefulness. Lamont was particularly keen on staring at me. But every now and then he'd suddenly look into the woods and mutter something I couldn't make out. But neither Aunt Sadie nor Doc seemed to notice; they were focused on their conversation.

After Lamont had looked off into the woods several times, I asked him:

— Lamont, what do you hear out there?

— Woods, he mumbled.

— Yes, I said. What's in the woods?

— Woods, he said again, somewhat clearer.

Then he pointed, now grinning and rocking back and forth. Pointing seemed to excite him, and he recommenced drooling and rocking harder, enough for Aunt Sadie to notice. She wiped his mouth and said:

— Now Lamont, calm yourself.

— Woods, he said again.

— Yes, we know about the woods. Now you be polite in front of your cousin Eva.

Well, that got me! I had no idea Lamont was my cousin. And I wasn't sure I wanted him to be. I thought I just called Aunt Sadie *Aunt* because she was an old friend of the family. But I know how to be polite too. I smiled again.

Then Lamont waved his big arms in no particular direction before motioning toward the woods again. I ducked, afraid he might accidentally clobber me. Aunt Sadie stood and gently pressed Lamont's hands into his lap. She looked at him, holding his hands a little longer, then turned to Doc. Lamont seemed to relax, but he started a quiet moaning and a slower, more hesitant rocking, still keeping his hands in his lap.

After that, Lamont seemed to forget I was there. He looked at his lap and towards the woods. If he heard something now, he didn't say anything or point. Aunt Sadie and Doc resumed their conversation. I listened harder now, trying to hear what Lamont heard, and a couple of times I thought I heard something too. Or maybe it was what Doc calls *sympathetic hearing*, when you think you hear something just because someone else hears it.

After we got home from Aunt Sadie's I met Billy in the barn loft. He wanted to hear about the visit. But I didn't want to talk about it. I didn't know what to make of Lamont's being my cousin. Doc hadn't explained it. He had been preoccupied and not very talkative.

I did mention Lamont to Billy because I wanted to tell him about something related that happened on the way home. Since Doc and I weren't rambling on the way we sometimes do, I'd gone into one of the mental journeys Poppy had taught me. And while I was picturing the crossroads store (that's one of the stops on that journey), I saw Lamont! He was younger, but his ears still stuck out from his short hair. He certainly hadn't been in my memory journey before. But there he was, walking down the outside stairs from the apartment above the store. Then I remembered that Uncle Charles had once lived above the store before he built his cabin on the edge of the woods. But I didn't see Charles in my memory journey, just Lamont. I tried to hold Lamont's image as long as I could, to see where it would take me, but eventually he faded out. That was when the idea came to me: the new game to create with Billy.

—I invented a new game on the way home.

—Another one? Billy said, getting up to join me where I was sitting cross-legged on a straw bale.

—Yes, but it's not finished. I need your help.

He laughed and straddled a bale facing me. He likes to be a part of inventing a game as well as playing it. And this particular game was going to be as much about inventing as playing.

—So what's the game?

—Well, that's the part I need your help with. And … calling it a game might not be entirely accurate.

—You're trying to confuse me. Just tell me the rules, and we'll play.

—That's just it. I don't know the rules.

He looked a bit hard at me, but I knew he wasn't upset, just curious.

—The idea came to me when we were driving home. I saw it during my memory journey. While I was imagining the crossroads store.

—OK, what's the idea?

—Suppose a game could be more than a few hands of cards or the time it takes to complete a trip around a board. Suppose the game extended into our lives, and we played it all the time.

—What kind of game is that? Games always have beginnings and endings.

—But suppose this one doesn't. What if you started playing, and it continued indefinitely.

—You mean like capture the flag? It can go forever if you have two good teams.

—Not exactly. I mean more like: It just keeps going day after day. The players continue playing even after they leave the board.

—There's a board?

—I'm not sure. It's the principle I'm trying to design.

—The principle?

—Call it the mood if you want. But let's say you play the game day after day. Each time a player sees another player, they remember where they are in the game. Each makes a move, and they go on. The next time they see each other, they continue from where they left off. That's how the game works.

—So who wins?

—That's another tricky part. I'm not really sure.

—Well, if there's no winning, is there losing?

—Possibly. But I haven't worked that out yet.

—What have you worked out? Why play? Who cares?

—That's the funny part. When I was at the store in my journey, I saw a group of people sitting in the back. Around a stove. Talking. I think they were a committee who decides things about the game.

—A committee? Were they making the rules?

—I don't think so. I think they mainly enforce the rules and decide who's ahead at any given time.

—Oh. Now this is getting interesting. A committee decides

who's ahead? But they don't know the rules.

—Well, they have to know the rules. And someone is a Supreme Leader or a Chief. He's the best player.

—Who decides that? The committee?

—Yes. That's part of their job: to decide who's the best.

—And what does the best player get to do?

—Nothing. He just keeps working on his game.

Billy sighed. That's another thing I like about him. When he's frustrated, he doesn't get mad, he just sighs as if to say, let's hear the rest of it.

—I'd been seeing Lamont on the outside stairs. Then I saw the committee inside. Yes (*I closed my eyes to concentrate*), it was four men and three women sitting around the stove. The long counter went along one side from front to back. And except for the light above the counter, which was reflected in the mirror behind the counter, it was dark.

—Any customers?

—I'm not sure.

—Then tell me more about the committee.

—Like I said, the committee decides things. I'm pretty sure other people are playing the game. Perhaps a lot of them! And the committee decides things about their games as well.

—Wait a minute. Is there one game? Or are there a lot of games?

—I think one game. But it consists of other games, sub-games maybe. That's why I need your help.

—Tell me again how you came up with this game?

—I saw it in a memory journey. A vision, Billy. So you can't expect me to know all the ins and outs.

—Well, suppose the committee was set up to choose who was playing well …

—Go on, I said.

—Let's say that the game has been going on for a long time. Skip the details for now, but suppose that the game got started, and more and more people began playing. Then something happened, and the game got out of hand. That's when they decided they needed someone, or say, a committee, to keep an

117

eye on things, to enforce the rules and settle disputes.

—Disputes?

—Sure, when you play a game someone is bound to break the rules. And that's where the committee comes in. They decide whether or not a rule has been broken and then make an appropriate decision.

—Like a judge and jury?

—Maybe. But more informally. Let's say that if you break a rule, you're not allowed to play any more.

—Oh, that's sad.

—Yes! Exactly. And that reduces the number of rule breakers. In fact, the committee becomes so powerful and there are so few rules breakers, that the committee's main job becomes choosing other members to replace themselves on the committee.

—And to choose the Supreme Leader!

—Yes. But ... hey, here's a switch. If you're a member of the committee, you can't become the Supreme Leader, ever. The committee can only choose the Supreme Leader from game players not on the committee.

—Why's that?

—To protect the integrity of the committee. Yes! (*Billy was rolling now.*) A member of the committee knows that he, or she, can't ever become the Supreme Leader. Once you're on the committee, you can only perfect your own game and supervise the players below you.

—So the committee consists of the best players.

—Yes, with one exception, the Supreme Leader, who is *the* best player. But the Supreme Leader can only become the best player *if* he isn't on the committee.

I had to think about Billy's variation. He'd come up with something more creative than I'd imagined. But it made sense. If you had no hope of becoming Supreme Leader, you could focus on your other duties. If you played well, you might make the committee. But if you played even better, you might become the best player. My head spun a little at the trick.

—Very clever, I said. How'd you come up with that?

—From my dad. He's says the problem with politicians

is they're mostly interested in bettering themselves. But if a committee member can't become more powerful than he already is, the only incentive would be to play the game well and help others do the same.

—What about the Supreme Leader?

—Good question …

He squinted for a moment, looking out the loft window. I looked too but didn't see anything. Then he licked his lips like he was deep in thought and said:

—It almost makes me sad to think of him. He's the best player and everyone knows it. But he doesn't get to decide anything.

After I'd helped Rosa peel potatoes and slice green tomatoes, I went upstairs. I pulled the rope, easing down the attic ladder, and unfolded the steps. They screeched and grunted as I locked them into place. Holding the oil lamp with one hand, I climbed. The boxes and crates were in disarray as Mama and Doc had been sorting through things to ship to Colorado.

I moved a few boxes, looking for a tea tin I'd hidden. That's when I noticed a box with a uniform on top: Charles'. I'd always loved looking at it but only in the attic. Mama told me never to bring it downstairs because it brought back hard memories for everyone. I moved it aside and found an old canteen and a leather journal. I'd seen them before but never looked closely. I opened the canteen and smelled: metallic, cold and musty. The journal was empty. Charles was never much into writing. I flipped through it, thinking that I would need a journal for our trip, and perhaps Charles would let me have this one. As I was considering how to ask him, a piece of paper slipped out. I unfolded it carefully.

July 20, 1918
Dear Charles,

The handwriting slanted naturally. I flipped the page.

Lovingly yours, Lily

Lily? A love letter? I wondered if Billy would write me.

I am writing to you with news. I hope you will take this well, though I know you have all the reason you need to be upset with me. Please know that I love you and want to be with you. I am at your farm. I didn't know where else to go. Your Poppy tells me the Allies are pushing the Germans back, and maybe this will mean the end of it all and you can come home.

Your mama made me promise to write you. She is very good to me.

Charles, I am carrying your baby. I know we only were together a few nights when you were at training camp. But it happened then, and your mama says all things happen for a reason. I know it's your baby. Your Poppy is real good to me too. They say I can stay here as long as I need to.

But I'll understand if you want me to go. My daddy kicked me out of the house when I told him. I'm showing, Charles, so I can't keep it a secret. Some girls told me how I could get rid of it, but I don't want to do that unless you want me to. I know it'll bring shame to you if others find out, seeing as we're not married. I'll keep myself a secret as long as I can. Your mama says they'll work something out, that I'm to stay here so she can help me. She'll take good care of me I know, but I don't want to burden you all. Plus, I've heard talk that you had a girlfriend in these parts, and I don't want to ruin things.

You just say the word, and I'll pick up and go. I took care of myself and my brothers after my mama died, so I know I'll be OK. I'll never tell anyone you're the father. I'll make up a story that he went to war and didn't come back.

Just tell me what you want me to do. I can be gone when you get back, if you want.

How could he? I thought. Why didn't he marry her? Then I'd have another cousin. I looked in the box for more letters. But all I saw were a few official-looking papers that didn't interest me.

I was about to put the letter back but thought twice. Poppy would tell me the truth. It's not a crime to read a letter you just happen upon. I read the date again: *July 20, 1918.* I thought about that and made my way downstairs to the pictures in the parlor.

There was the picture of Mama, Doc, and Charles. I'd always assumed it was a wedding picture, but now I realized I wasn't even sure where it was or when exactly it had been taken. I tried to read Charles' face: hard and soft at the same time and not quite looking at the camera. He could have been a groom too if he'd made a better choice. He was so stubborn. How could someone you think you know and love so much have done something so terrible?

She found Poppy in the back field mending fence.

—Poppy. (*She looked at him, then away toward the woods.*) Can I ask you something?

—Eva, my darling, you can ask me anything.

—I found something.

She handed him the letter which he accepted and read while she continued.

—I found it in the attic. I know I should have left it, but I … Did Charles tell his girlfriend to leave? Do I have a … Does he have a child somewhere? (*Her face was red with tears and frustration.*) Did he abandon them? Because he had another girlfriend, or didn't want the trouble? Why didn't you make him marry her? You took care of her.

Poppy folded the letter and said:

—Some things that happened long ago aren't easy for us to understand now.

—But some things never change.

—Yes and no. Things can appear as they always were, but their associations and the meanings we attach to them change. And that's enough to make a new world.

She stared blankly into the woods and said:

—He didn't make her get rid of it, did he?

—Eva, it *is* about time you learned about this. But not just now. (*He put his arm around her and guided her toward the house.*) Rosa will have supper ready soon. Be patient, and ... I'll show you tomorrow. Your uncle didn't ask her to terminate her pregnancy, if that's what you need to know. He saw and experienced more death in that war than anyone ever should. They all did. Now it's getting dark. Let's go in, and I'll explain everything in the morning.

When Tesi recovered, Cerimon humbly presented her with the robe that had once cocooned her.

—I am forever in your debt, he told her solemnly.

But her eyes conveyed confusion. So Cerimon continued.

—Too hastily, I had thought your loved ones let you fly. But it was I, who too hastily dispensed with your robe. Dear one, your secret names. They are revealed.

He spread the robe across the stone floor of his chamber, and Tesi silently fingered the images carved and painted into the interior side of the robe. Cerimon said:

—Do you know what this means?

Tesi nodded, but then shook her head slowly. She said:

—The sacred names, these are about me? But once the secret is revealed, the soul—I?—am I earthbound?

—The figure is clearly you, Cerimon said. Feel your ears. Do you not feel the three stones in your left, the two in your right? Do you not see them there in the figure with the stag above it?

Tesi ran her fingers over the five stones pierced into her ears.

— But then I am … lost? Until …

— I should have let you await your loved ones in the womb of Mother Earth. Now, with your secrets revealed, only when you are reunited will you know yourself again.

— I do not … know myself. I do not, remember. I do not, understand.

Tears welled in her eyes, and Cerimon eased down to kneel beside her.

— Study the images, he said. Be with them. Meditate on them. One to the other and to the next. Breathe. Follow the path, and you may find understanding.

Cerimon left her to consider the pictures in solitude.

— A deer? she said to herself. Myself? The one from the west, where the wind blows free. Like the berries, the bark, the herbs and seeds that deer feed on … I, too, nourish the people? Gentle, peace-loving. Fearless to sacrifice self, so that the family stays united.

She remembered the meanings of the symbols, but … She shook her head. *What have I done?*

When she removed her tear dampened hands from her face, she fingered the spirals that were painted to the left of the figure that represented her.

— Whirlwind. My parentage was like the wind, a channel of communication to the Great Spirit, enlightened. He who gathers information and disperses it. One whose imagination finds new truths. In the sky, he is the Lord of the Dance, around which the Heavens whirl in a never ending ring.

Above the spirals an ear of corn, five kidney-shaped beans, and a long-necked squash had been etched. The image on the other side of her figure was topped with another ear of corn, five corn kernels, and an oblong shape representing grinding stone. She traced the curved pointed shape below the corn. Over an over, she traced it, searching.

— Rattlesnake tooth, she finally said. What wise one has attached himself to me? What priest? Or magician? Shaman? Or … sorcerer? But as she closed her eyes, she saw a rainbow in her mind, glowing forth from a foggy riverbank.

—Rattlesnake tooth, she said again, turning her eyes to the image, her hand holding the tooth that Cerimon had given her. Daylight and dark night, come together in you, rainbow, sky symbol of the rattlesnake tooth. Serene, clairvoyant. But deep within a fragile feather. Ever torn between one breeze and the other. The people. The everlasting life of the imagination. Which did you choose? But we ... (*her eyes turned to the image below hers*) we chose a child? Who is this red bird? Sweet red bird ...

Tesi cradled a warmth in her arms, imagining a babe.

—Red bird, she sang sweetly. Friend of the dream world. Innocent child. All love and beauty, but ... without a mother.

Tears poured down her cheeks, and Tesi could not be comforted. Day after day she studied the images, one to the next, always in the same order, but she could not conjure the memories. *A father, a husband, a daughter, a life ... lost.* She resolved to devote what remained of her life to prayer and meditation.

So Cerimon led her to the Temple of Ayla, a great glittering cavern deep beneath an old oak grove. There dwelt the spirit of Ayla, the guardian of the earth, the hunt, the woodlands, and the moon. And there Tesi devoted herself to prayer, releasing her sorrows to Ayla.

Reed

Kansas is dry as a bone, with fields of shriveled wheat and corn and creeks running nowhere. In the dim light the landscape looks like a weathered photograph in brittle grays and browns. In Virginia mist rises from the fields at daybreak. But here only rivers suggest rain. I remember what Billy said about the desert, and I wonder how dry it will get before we reach Django.

Dawn, O day. Mama knits, humming another Bartók tune she likes to play. We only had a few hours of sleep, but we're all awake as if expecting something to happen. The farmers out here must feel that way, hoping for rain each morning.

I ask Mama:

—How do people survive in this country?

—Out here, honey, it's not easy. Even in the best of times. Many families have moved.

—Where?

—Wherever they can find jobs. Or have family to help them. If you don't have somewhere to be, you need somewhere to go.

Near the train a cloud of dust rises and spins out of nowhere.

—Dust devil, Doc says.

At our next stop, Dodge City, a few hodgepodge families board the train: a young man who can't be much older than Billy carries a baby, a man and woman with two small children at their heels, and an older man with a younger woman helping him. My guidebook says Dodge City was the wickedest town in the Wild West. But it looks far from wicked now. The streets are deserted.

Three men, standing apart from one another on the platform, wave goodbye to faces in the windows of the train. I imagine wives, children, friends. Things were better in Virginia, and I can't understand why we left.

Dawn at home, Monte, our ebony cock, was crowing. I lay in bed listening and picturing him until I heard Poppy whisper:
— Eva.

I sat up as he opened the door. I was worried that something was wrong. He put his finger across his lips and motioned for me to follow.
— Dress warmly, he said.

A few minutes later I found him outside.
— I promised to show you something. We'll be back by breakfast.

We waded through the wet grasses, goldenrod, mullein, asters. The light rose from the mist as we climbed to the place where the old wagon trail splits off and goes toward the church.
— Are we going to church?
— Not exactly. But that's our direction.

As the church came in sight, Poppy turned toward the cemetery. The mist hugged the ground, and I imagined a ghost shimmering above the gate. I shivered, not that I'd had any experience of ghosts (*that I knew of for sure*), but I'd heard ghosts come to cemeteries just before sunrise. I looked at Poppy who was looking at me.

I followed him to a cluster of gravestones surrounding a black oak. Leaves covered the ground. This was where Rosa went when she tended the family graves.
— Why are we here?
— Let's look around, Poppy said.

He stopped by a small limestone marker.
— Here, he said.

I had to kneel beside it to read the inscription.

Iris Walton
Nov 6, 1840 – Oct 3, 1922
By that God we both adore

I said:

—That's my great-grandmother Iris, your mother. She died of pneumonia when I was one. You told me that.

—You have an excellent memory. And this one?

I knelt to read a smaller stone:

Ave Walton
Dec 1, 1918 – Oct 1, 1922
Be that word our sign of parting

—Ave?

My Ave? The air seemed to stop. I couldn't breathe. What was happening? She would have been three years older than me.

—Was she my cousin?

Poppy motioned to another gravestone:

Lily
1901 – Dec 1, 1918
Leave my loneliness unbroken

—Ave's mother? She … died in childbirth?

—Influenza. It ravaged the whole county that fall.

—Why haven't you told me about them?

—We decided, Poppy said slowly, that it was best to bury that part of the past.

How could they?
I perched alone and cold.

How could they not tell me about Ave?
And Lily.
A world of secrets all around me.

The ones I knew, that I loved,
that I assumed loved me,
were the ones not telling me.

Why did we have to leave so soon? Doc said we needed to get settled before bad weather set in.

—Where we're going, snowstorms can occur any time. We have to be ready.

But it didn't feel like snow. What was the hurry?
I wanted to be here, right here. Right here on the farm.

I could feel her body warm beside me.
When she tapped my forehead I opened my eyes.

I was at the river. Doc held me in his arms.
—Say goodbye to your great-grandmother, Eva.

I reached for her and searched for words, my mouth confused:
—I ce, I is, I sis.

She blew me a kiss
Snow *was* falling

Everything was
Moving around me

I tried to stretch my arms, wanting to touch her, but I couldn't. Was I dying?

In Two Rivers, Manki and Mihani raised Marina with their daughter, Witēka (which means *daughter*). Marina and Witēka played together and loved each other like sisters. They learned the fine arts of weaving, singing, and flute playing, and both excelled. But Marina was more widely praised. The people remembered and loved her father who had once saved them from famine. Now their love grew and included his daughter.

Mihani had been Marina's proud surrogate mother, but as Marina grew old enough to marry and the people wondered who among them would become her husband, Mihani raged. She expected Witēka to be the center of such attention and determined that Marina must be removed.

After Marina's nurse Mayen died unexpectedly, Mihani sent for her servant, Little Ant, and commanded him to meet her in the sacred meadow.

In a hushed, stern voice, she said:

— You will take Marina's life.

— What? I mistake you, my lady.

— You mistake me not. Do as I say or die with her yourself.

— Why?

— She has disobeyed me.

Marina appeared in the meadow while Little Ant and Mihani discussed her death. Marina was collecting wildflowers for Mayen's grave. When Little Ant saw Marina, he said to Mihani:

— My lady, I cannot do it.

But Mihani's eyes silenced him.

Mihani walked toward a tearful Marina and chided her for showing her emotions.

— What will your father think of how we've raised you?

— My father? Is there news?

— I didn't want to spoil the surprise. But yes, we are expecting him soon. Now go with Little Ant, and he will prepare you for your father's arrival.

She took Marina's flowers.

— I will care for these. Go.

To Little Ant, she said calmly:

—I'll expect you promptly.

Little Ant walked away with Marina. While they walked, she told him of her frightful birth on the river. Little Ant, full of more pity than he could deal with, knew he must kill her quickly before he lost his nerve.

—Marina, say your prayers.

Marina was confused.

—And quickly too.

—But Little Ant, why do you act so strangely?

—I must do this quickly.

—What? Harm me? But why?

—I have been ordered by Mihani.

—But I have never betrayed Mihani. I have only honored her and have hurt neither fly nor flower.

—It is not my job to reason but to act.

Little Ant stepped toward Marina with his knife raised.

—Oh Ayla, Marina called out. Protect me!

And before Little Ant could strike, he was pulled to the ground by three rowdy river men that had come up from the bank.

—What have we here? one said, eying Marina. A beauty. She'll sell for a good price. Tie them up, but leave the ugly one here.

They bound Marina, took her to their canoes, and started downriver.

Meanwhile, Little Ant untied himself and realized his good fortune. He would tell Mihani that he threw Marina into the river after he took her life.

Panther

$\mathcal{S}$omewhere near the Colorado border I think I see the Rocky Mountains in the distance. Then they disappear.

— Keep looking, Mama says. They're out there, but sometimes they look like clouds.

She pulls a small oval mirror from her purse and disappears into it. That reminds me of Halloween and the lady's voice and the band playing as we reached the front porch of the Potter's house. A feathery mask held to her face, Mrs. Potter greeted us:

— Hallow. Come into my parlor, said the spider to the fly.

I pretended to laugh, but I admit she spooked me a little.

Mrs. Potter took our coats, and she and Mama began to talk. Doc joined a group of men around a wood stove, and I was left on my own in the entryway in front of a full-length mirror. It filled most of the wall to the right of the door and reflected the opposite wall, on which hung an oval mirror not much larger than my face. It contained my face. The mirrors reflected each other, sending me into infinity.

The entryway was dark except for six candles, three each on two small tables against opposite walls. I remembered the superstition Aunt Katie had told me about. If you gaze into a mirror on Halloween night, your future husband's face will appear. I thought it was worth a try, and no one was paying any attention to me anyhow.

So I stood very still, relaxing my breath, looking into the long mirror and through it to the oval mirror. A few minutes went by. I stood patiently, listening to the piano and Nathaniel's cousin, Ella, singing the blues. Then the music seemed to come from far away, and I knew I was seeing something change behind me in the mirror across the entryway. A face appeared flickering in the candlelight. It *was* a boy's face. Or a man's. I couldn't tell which. The image shimmered there a few seconds, then was gone. I didn't recognize the face. But I knew it wasn't Billy.

Leaving the mirrors, Eva went into the main room where Doc and Edmund had started a chess game in one corner. Doc loved chess, and he'd taught Eva to play before she started school. But that night Eva didn't feel like sitting with them. Still, she wanted to watch, so she stood in the stairway where they wouldn't notice her. A pair of candles lit the board, shadowing the men.

Edmund won the draw and played white.

EDMUND: Pawn to e4.
DOC: Pawn to d5.

— Ah, the Scandinavian Defence. That's an old one, Doc.
— If it works, no need to fix it.
— That's a thought, but I'm going to bet your defense is broken before it even gets started.

EDMUND: Pawn takes pawn.
DOC: Knight to f6.

Edmund said:
— Well, now. A willingness to sacrifice a pawn to undermine my center. I suppose you think you'll get that pawn back later. But I'm not so sure.

EDMUND: Pawn to c4.
DOC: Pawn to c6.

Eva stepped closer to get a better view of the board. Edmund looked up at her. His eyes twinkled, and he grinned as he turned to Doc, whose back was to Eva. She quickly stepped into the stairway and crouched on the second step, looking out between the railings.

EDMUND: Pawn takes pawn.
DOC: Knight takes pawn.

—And now I believe I'm up that pawn, Doc, and your little sacrifice won't amount to much.

Eva was surprised by Doc's poor play. She knew Edmund was a good player, and giving him a pawn so early in the game would make things even more difficult later.

The men took their time between moves, neither talking.

EDMUND: Pawn to d3.
DOC: Pawn to e5.
EDMUND: Knight to c3.
DOC: Bishop to c5.
EDMUND: Bishop to g5.
DOC: Castle.

—A little late to be playing defense, don't you think, Doc?
—Some say a good offense is a good defense.
—You're old-fashioned, behind the times. You know it. I know it.

EDMUND: Knight to e4.

—And I believe the center is mine again, Doc.

DOC: Knight (f6) x Knight (e4).

—My, my. Are you playing to lose? Surely, you're not going to sacrifice your queen too?
—You don't have to take it.

133

—Oh, but I believe I do, Edmund chuckled.

EDMUND: Bishop x Queen (d8).

Eva was stunned. Doc had lost his queen. That was enough. She didn't want to listen while Edmund gloated. She turned up the stairs toward the nursery. She'd find Rachael to talk to.

DOC: Bishop x Pawn (f2). Check.

Edmund's smile vanished.
—What's this? he said.
—A little something I thought you might appreciate.

EDMUND: King e2.
DOC: Knight d4.

Edmund looked at the board in disbelief. Doc said:
—I believe that's checkmate. Or as some folks call it, a *reverse legal's mate*.
Edmund searched the board for an answer, but of course none was coming. He said angrily:
—You might have won the game, but the game is not life. I've said all along, play your part in the life going on around you. I'm still willing to have you on board.
Doc kept his eyes on the pieces.
—The life you think is going on all around you isn't the life I want. You're trying to break up my family.
Edmund glared.
—You're breaking the law! You broke the law. I've been breaking the law to cover your hide. You owe me.
—Let's not start this again, Doc said, shaking his head. Laws—moral, political, or otherwise—it all depends on your perspective.
—The scientific evidence—
—Biased. I know the *studies* you're referring to. I read them too, and we both know there's more speculation than truth.

—Don't be high and mighty with me. You choose to see what you want same as I do. Of course your own bias would lead you to find nothing wrong with members of your own family. Why even that boy, Lamont. Consider that. You see him as gifted, is that correct?

—I'm not talking about Lamont.

—Oh, I know, but tell me—

—But since you bring him up, Lamont wouldn't hurt a soul. And he's not out there spreading his genes around like you're so worried he might.

—It's for his own safety. For *all* our safety. Plus, think of what we could learn from studying him that could help others like him.

—Electrocuting people and opening up their heads is not therapy.

—Light shock treatments have known benefits. And that's not all we're doing.

—You make me sick.

—I'm going to be a rich man whether you like it or not.

—Is money all you think about?

—Of course not. There's honor, distinction, and don't forget the scientific achievement. And it could be yours too. This knowledge will help the unfortunate far into the future. And you can be a part of it. Or you can see what it really means to separate a family when you're behind bars. The government doesn't look kindly on forging legal documents, does it? And then we'd have to find these missing persons, wouldn't we? The safe haven you *think* you created for them, which I fear is not in their best interests, would have to be divulged, now wouldn't it? Otherwise the rest of your family could be seen as accomplices. And your daughter … without parents or grandparents, or sane relatives. I know about that aunt of yours. We'd take good care of her too.

—I can assure you, that won't happen.

—Well, I'm also the one in charge, aren't I? And with you around, my hospital suffers. People think you're smart, that you give them better service. But you're just young and old-fashioned. Your head's in the past. New ideas are what the people need, not someone telling them it's OK to keep to the old ways. And even you'd agree that the innocent people in our county do not want anyone hiding menaces from them.

—Menaces, Edmund? Really, is that what you think of anyone who's different from you? Who might not have had your advantages. Or maybe they scare you? That my grandmother had a habit of disappearing? That she could heal the sick better than you? That's what bothers you about traditional ways, isn't it?

—Your niece was absolutely abnormal.

—Abnormal? Because she didn't feel like talking yet? She wasn't even four years old.

—More like she *couldn't* talk, and instead, she did unnatural things. Clear signs of early stage schizophrenia. Mental deterioration *in utero* due to maternal influenza. These cases are well documented. Hers was another clear case: mother had influenza, went into labor early. The child was sick. You're just denying the facts.

—She simply had skills you didn't understand.

—Oh, a witch, was she? It's the twentieth century! I'm beginning to think you might need treatment. And tell me, are there others? With these special gifts, as you call them? If there are, you know where they belong. We'd take good care of them. We're doctors, for God's sake. And confining their genes is for the betterment of our entire race, not just our little county. This is bigger than you realize. For generations to come, societies to come. The fate of our species lies in acting on scientific data, not ignoring it or trying to cover it up!

Edmund had gotten louder, and several people looked up from elsewhere in the room. From the upstairs nursery, Eva thought she heard something about race and covering up something. She tiptoed down the stairs, trying to get close enough to hear. But Edmund had stopped talking, and Doc spoke too quietly for Eva to hear.

—Tell me, I recall your pappy had a problem with the jug, same as you. And your son, he never was up to much good, now was he? I suppose that's direct evidence, isn't it? I figure you might want to castrate him.

—You're barking up the wrong tree. Remember who's committed the crime according to *our* laws. You signed the documents. If we dig up those graves (*Edmund continued in a hushed tone*), I know what we'll find. And we'll eventually find your *safe haven*. We have the weight of the law behind us.

—You will never find them.

—Well, maybe not. But we'll make the Walton clan miserable in the meantime. Your granddaddy wasn't too smart marrying in with those funny types.

&

Chick arrived in Two Rivers soon after Marina's departure. Manki was disgusted with his wife's actions, but he played the lie. He and Mihani led Chick to the monument they had erected for Marina's memorial. A funeral had been staged, alleging that Marina had died in the night of an unknown cause. Because of rapid deterioration of her body from the sudden illness, they chose not to show it.

Chick was horrified. His last hope had vanished, and he sank into a deep melancholy. His misery was so great that he determined never to speak again. His good friend Wink was there to care for him. Chick merely drifted now, a lost soul. Once more, they loaded their canoes and started back down the Sacred River toward their home along the Chickahominy.

Meanwhile, Marina's kidnappers had sold her into slavery downriver in the Hill City, where her unusual gifts were soon recognized; she progressed from menial labor to teaching the fine arts. She made her masters rich by entertaining visitors with her music and dancing. The Hill City people admired her. The chief's son, Ipikam, named for his handsome features, secretly wished that he might marry her. However, whenever he asked her about her parentage, she burst into tears and would not speak of it.

Eagle

The Arkansas River twists and bends through the plains as the sun rises behind us. We have scrambled eggs and toast with jam for breakfast. Then we go to the observation car. Mama sits with me, and Doc works across the aisle, a pile of papers on his lap. The cottonwoods and willows shine golden along the riverbanks. A large bird soars above the river.

—Is that a …? I say, pointing.

Mama leans across me.

—Bald eagle. It must be looking for fish.

—It fishes from up there?

—Eagles have great eyes. They see far away details that we can't. There'll be lots of eagles in Colorado. Goldens as well.

When it dives, I lose sight of it. But it reappears, with something in its talons. Everything out here is wild.

Doc says:

—A country with grit, and I mean that in the best sense. You're going to like it, Eva.

Bunch grasses are dry and parched. One plant seems to thrive: sword-shaped leaves clustering into a pincushion like a porcupine, two or three feet tall.

—Yucca, Doc says when I ask.

We're coming into La Junta. I turn to Mama.

—What does La Junta mean?

—Do you mean La Junta? she says, pronouncing the J like an H.

—La Hoonta?

—*Yah, La Junta. Aber … ich weiss nicht.*

She winks, and I know it means *I don't know*.

—I'll be right back, she says getting up.

I whisper, *La Junta,* making the J sound like an H. But is it *hoonta* or *hunta*?

Mama returns with a little red book.

—I had a feeling you'd want to know what all the Spanish names meant. So I found this for you at the bookstore in Chicago.

—*A Basic List of Spanish Words and Idioms.* Mama! It's perfect. Thank you. *Danke.*

—*Bitte,* she says. It's from your father too. We'll count on you to translate for us.

—I will! Do you want to know what *La Junta* means?

—I do.

I flip pages until I find *junta.*

—Meeting, conference, council. And (*I skim farther down*) *juntar* means to join, unite. *Junto*—joined, united. *Juntura*—a junction. Do you suppose this was a meeting place, maybe a secret council? It feels like the middle of nowhere.

—The middle of nowhere, Mama says, but perhaps on the way to many places.

Doc says:

—You two look serious. Did I miss a secret powwow?

I laugh.

—No, we're just wondering why they call La Junta La Junta. Thanks for the dictionary.

I show him the book.

—So educate me.

—La means *the.* So La Junta means *the joining place.* But it's in the middle of nowhere! But maybe on the way to somewhere? Like Denver? Not to mention, Santa Fe.

—Next stop, La Junta, the conductor calls. A ten minute break. Don't wander off. La Junta, gateway to Colorado.

—Can we? I ask Doc.

—If we're quick as lightning. Just a peek inside the station, then right back.

—Hold this for me? I ask Mama, handing her my new

dictionary.
—Of course.
I pick up my journal and hurry to catch Doc.
Outside people are loading and unloading, suitcases and trunks. But only a few people get off. We enter the tiny station. A poster of a log cabin with mountains in the distance is titled: *La Junta: Where the Santa Fe Trail Divides.*
I barely have time to look around when Doc says:
—Time to board.
The conductor, one hand cupped beside his mouth, shouts:
—All abo'rd, All abo'rd. Bound for Trinidad.
In the middle of nowhere. Or thereabouts.

The train takes us to the foot of the mountains.

Trinidad.
The holy trinity?
I check my dictionary.

Trino, trill, singing.
Towhees singing
back home.

tow he e
drink your
tea e

They have bright rusty breasts
and scratch the dirt for food.

El Rio de Las Animas en Purgatorio runs south to north through Trinidad.

EAGLE

Rio river
Anima soul

ghosts

sail down
to eternity.

The Purgatoire River got its name from the Spanish conquistadors who were searching for the Seven Cities of Gold. 1594. They were crazy for gold and forced the Indians to dig for it. And when they were through with their Indian slaves, killed them. Later, according to legend, the conquistadors were attacked, killed, and spent an eternity in purgatory paying for their crimes.

But how can you have *spent* an eternity? If it's eternity, it's never completed.

And what was is that Edmund said? *Remember who committed the crime.* Did I really hear that? Or imagine it.

We cross an iron bridge over the Purgatoire. The rivers are getting smaller; this one isn't much wider than Mill Creek. I stare at the sky reflected in the water and think.

A crisp morning, that Wednesday, *Eagle*. A week ago yesterday. Feels like a lifetime ago, yet somehow only yesterday … at the same time.

I heard a light knock on my door. I had been awake a while, had dressed, then crawled back under the quilt to savor the warmth.

—Coming, I said.

I knew it would be Poppy. After he showed me the graves, he said he'd explain everything soon. We would start by honoring one of Rosa's family traditions the day after Halloween. *To remember those who've gone before us. Those on the other side of the veil.*

But it wasn't Poppy who opened the door.

—Mama?

She was wearing her long wool skirt and handed me a thick shawl.

—You'll need this. It's cold out this morning.

—Are you coming too?

—Our traditions in Austria were not so different than Rosa's.

She wrapped the shawl around my head.

—Too tight!

—Can you breathe?

I sighed as she wrapped me into a cocoon.

—Catching a cold is the last thing you need before traveling. Don't forget your mittens.

Poppy and Rosa were waiting in the kitchen. Rosa handed me a cup of hot tea and a thin biscuit.

—This will warm you. Then we can go.

It was still dark as we walked through the frosty fields. Ice sparkled. Mama carried a basket of the beeswax candles we'd dipped last winter. Kleela walked ahead as if she knew where we were going, and this time I also knew.

—My granny called it *Samhain*, Rosa said as we reached the cemetery gate. Summer's end.

—Which means it's also a beginning, Poppy said. Every time something ends, something begins.

Mama took my hand, and we walked to the gravestones Poppy had shown me earlier.

—Dig a very small hole with this trowel, Mama said. Then I'll put in a candle.

Mama lit one candle, then turned an unlit wick into the flame and secured the newly lit candle into the hole I'd prepared. We did this at a dozen or more graves until the cemetery glowed. Mama's eyes were misting, and I wondered what, or who, she was remembering. I took her hand again.

Rosa and Poppy were beside us now, and Rosa said:

—That's a beautiful sight. Rest assured, the veil is lifted. We honor those who've gone before us. We remember.

I knelt beside Ave's grave. I tried to remember ... a girl playing with her baby cousin, me. Did she shake a rattle or show me a doll? Was any of this possible? How much of this was I making up? How much was real?

—Tell me something about Ave, I said, looking up at Mama.

Mama looked at Poppy who said:

—Close your eyes. Picture a wisp of a girl, lighter than a feather, who never spoke. But in your mind, you could hear her singing. She loved to listen to Leah playing. She danced and clapped her little hands. And then she'd disappear, as if she'd never been there.

Rosa said:

—She loved you, Eva. She knew you were a gift. She'd watch over you in your crib while you slept. I know she *whispered* to you. But none of the rest of us ever heard her talk. She was so careful with you, as if she were afraid you'd break.

Mama sat next to me and pulled me close.

—I'd hold Ave just as I'm holding you. And she held you. She'd kiss and stroke your skin as lightly as if she were touching the petals of a rose.

Mama caressed my hair and pulled it back around my ears. Slowly the sun evaporated the frost, and the candles grew dim. Mama said:

—Why don't you put what's left of the candles in the basket?

I carefully extinguished each candle, licking my thumb and forefinger and letting the wick sizzle between them. I saved Ave's for last. She'd have been almost four; I was only a year old. So long ago, and my memories of that time so dim. Why? What did that mean? Would I ever know all the answers?

I'll never forget you, Ave. And I know you can hear me. I know you are here.

As I was latching the cemetery gate, I thought I heard someone say my name. I looked back into the cemetery and up the hill. Mama and Poppy and Rosa had already started down. The light in the trees caught my eye, and a red maple leaf danced to the ground. I heard it again … *Eva*. A flutter of wings.

Handsome Ipikam noticed a line of canoes gliding around one of the many islands in the river at the base of the Hill City. He sent a messenger out to greet them. Wink was delighted with the warm reception and ordered the canoes ashore.

There Wink explained to Ipikam:

— My master has lost his speech. He grieves in silence.

Ipikam tried talking to Chick, who stared past him. Ipikam said to Wink:

— I will summon a girl who can surely draw your master from his sadness. She is the pride of our city, and her voice is an angel's. She will enchant even your grieving friend.

Wink and Chick's men were resting in a grove of sycamores when Ipikam returned with Marina. She walked to where Chick sat alone. Head bent loosely, his hair was matted around his face. Marina sat beside him and began to sing softly. She enunciated each word, each note as if she were a heavenly bird, a thrush, or a wren. But Chick did not even raise his eyes to her.

Marina said softly:

— I have a story as sad or sadder than yours, and yet I do not weep. How can you resist the voice of a young woman? You, who could be a father. I lost my father long ago.

Chick's eyelids opened to a slit, his eyes still deep in darkness.

She said:

— I tell you my story is true and one to be wept over too.

Chick tilted his head slightly toward her, and that was enough for Marina to tell him the story of how she was separated from her family and sold into slavery. As she spoke, providing as much detail as she could remember, she became aware that Chick was listening. When she had stopped talking, they sat in silence for a while. Then Chick, who had hardly spoken to anyone, whispered almost inaudibly:

— What is your name?

— Marina.

— You ... mock me! Chick growled, now looking at her

closely. An unusual name, unusual circumstances. Please do not torment me.

— I do not. That is my name, given me at my birth during a great flood, so severe it was as if the sea overflowed the land.

— And who is your mother who bore you?

— The daughter of a chief.

— It cannot be. And your father?

— My father. I am told he is a priest of the Chickahominy.

— Tell me, what was your mother's name?

— My mother was called Tesi. She died the minute I began.

Chick realized he was seeing his daughter. He stood, overwhelmed with emotions he had thought forever buried, and he drew his daughter to her feet.

— It cannot be, he said.

Then he called to Wink:

— Come, my great friend. This is my daughter whom we thought dead.

Marina stood back and looked on Chick in wonder. Her father?

And looking into the sky, the trees, Chick said:

— What beautiful melodies. From where do they come?

Wink responded hesitantly:

— We hear no such music.

— Oh, but it is so beautiful.

Wink said to the others:

— He hears the music of the spheres. Let him believe we hear it too.

Owl

I replay the times I heard Ave calling my name … in the cemetery, at my lookout on the rocks, in the forest, outside my bedroom window. My ears pulse with trying to remember the sounds, and I press my hands against my head and close my eyes. My head throbs.

Doc says:

— Here, drink some water.

I open my eyes. I *am* thirsty.

— Ears hurt? he says.

— How did you know?

— I can feel it too. We're getting on up toward Raton Pass. Mama's the only one of us who's ever been this high.

— How high are we?

— The pass is seventy-eight hundred feet or more. Twice as high as anywhere you've been.

— How high is Django?

— Not as high. But high enough. You'll get used to it. Drink more water. The swallowing should help. I'll get you some crackers from the dining car.

As we wind our way up, the train slows, chugging through pines and juniper. I hear a jay squawk; its blue feathers glide between branches. I look back and can see most of the train all at once because of the curve in the track. I count sixteen cars, then close my eyes to avoid getting dizzier. My head spins like a top.

I remember the last day I waited for Ave at my lookout. The sun would set soon, so I knew I couldn't wait long for something to happen. A light breeze spun a maple leaf still clinging to an almost bare branch. The colors were muted, no longer the sunny pastels of a few weeks earlier. Can a leaf be sad that it won't dance again in a summer breeze?

I loosened my shawl and closed my eyes. Kleela pawed the ground and circled until she found her place to lie. I heard the thrush calling from somewhere far and high: *E-o-ah, Eee-vaa.*

I eat the crackers Doc brings me. I close my eyes and let the images reel through my mind. Trees drift past, and I fly through the darkness like an owl. Again I remember that last day at the lookout. Eyes closed, I was warm in strong arms, and I saw Poppy's face near mine. He winked, then kissed my nose and lowered me at the seep. I patted the water with my hand. Cold. Poppy cupped his hands and held them near my lips. I sipped the sweet water.

I sense the darkness of a tunnel. I feel like I'm falling, but my arms twitch and jolt me out of the dream. And I remember. I heard the rush of rapids and looked up to see Charles carrying a little girl as he stepped into the river. He handed her to a tall woman I knew was Iris. Her hair, long and silver, glistened iridescent like a raven's feathers. I knew it was Ave, who clung to Iris as she waded across the river and stepped out on the far bank. The snow was falling. I felt it melt as it touched my face.

I wasn't sure where I was. Mama was there. I was crying. She held me in her arms, rocking back and forth. I was so sleepy. I wanted to keep watching, to see everything that happened. But I couldn't.

While Chick slept Ayla appeared to him.

—Visit my temple in the mountain, she said. Offer your story to the priestesses there, and you will find peace.

While Chick slept, Ipikam professed his love to Marina. The next morning they came to Chick and asked for his blessings for their marriage.

Chick was stunned at the thought of losing his daughter so soon after finding her and felt anger rising. But he quickly regained control. In his heart he knew he wasn't losing Marina; he was recovering a family.

— Yes, he said. My blessings to you both. But first we must go to the Temple of Ayla.

Heron

another sandy riverbank
the trees explode
in fiery leaves

—How many? Doc asks.
—Rivers?
—Yes.
—Let's see ... If we start from home, there's the South and
the Maury, then the Jackson where we caught the train. Then the
New River and the Ohio, but I missed that one. I should have
stayed awake. That's five. And then I'm sure about the ones from
Chicago on: Chicago, Fox, Mississippi, Des Moines (and all those
other tributaries of the Mississippi, but we won't count them);
that's four, so nine. Then Missouri, Kansas, Arkansas, Purgatoire,
and now the Pecos. Five more, that makes fourteen. Did I miss
any?
—If you did, I did too. You'll get one more when we get to
Django.
—Which one?
—The Animas.
—Another *Animas*?
—*Rio de las Animas Perdidas*.
I check my dictionary ... River of Lost Souls? I wonder whose
souls were lost. What does it mean to be a lost soul? Does the
soul wander in purgatory, unable to find heaven or hell? Maybe
afraid of what it might find if it looks too closely? Rosa says we
must never lose touch with the souls that have gone before us. If
we lose touch, do souls become lost?

I think about Ave. I think about Billy. Will I see them again?

Light snow blew around Billy and me as we walked home. It had been my last day of school. I had handed in my last homework assignment. I thought about the assignment Poppy had given me:

> Remember each of these twenty days.
> Don't think of them as last days,
> but one turn in the cycle, one turn of the wheel.
> Etch as many details into your mind as you can.
> Then write them down in your journal.

Remember what Poppy said. The Day Memory System. Use an image for each day. Natural images, especially animals are the most memorable: Turtle, Whirlwind, Hearth, Serpent, Dragon, Twins, Deer, Rabbit, The River, Wolf, Raccoon, Rattlesnake Tooth, Reed, Panther, Eagle, Owl, Heron.

—Put them on a journey, I murmured.

—What? Billy said.

—Oh … I was just remembering when we looked for the haunted cabin.

—It was really there!

I laughed.

—Maybe.

He took my hand.

—Let's go up to the lookout.

—OK, I said.

—I'll run your books up to the house.

—I'll race you, I said handing him my books and running ahead.

—Hey, no fair!

We were both laughing when we reached the kitchen door. I'm not sure who got there first, but it didn't matter.

—Rosa, we're going up the hill, I panted.

Billy took my hand, and we ran back to the road. We slowed as we climbed the hill. I felt a little guilty for hurrying off. But I wanted this time with Billy, and it was starting to snow. Mama probably wouldn't even want me to be outside. But the sun was still shining, and I'd point that out if she reprimanded me later.

Billy reached the rocks first. He climbed up and held his hand down to me.

—You're frozen, he said and rubbed my arms.

And he kept me in his arms.

Snow and sunlight. The crystal flakes danced down but melted before they kissed the ground. The temperature was dropping, but I was warm, my head resting on Billy's shoulder.

—Have you seen the girl anymore?

—Ave? I think I've figured it out ... She must be a ghost.

—A ghost? Why? Are you sure?

—You think ghosts exist, right?

—I think so. But how can you be sure?

—I think it must have been the spirit of my cousin, Ave. We visited the cemetery, and it makes sense. She died on October first in 1922. I thought I had made up her name, but I must have pulled it out of my memory without realizing it. She was three years older than I was. I don't remember anyone ever talking to me about her before. But it was Samhain, the day of remembrance; I guess they felt it was time I knew. Anyhow, they said she didn't talk. She would have been almost four when she died. That must be the girl I see.

—Do you think you could be recalling memories? And somehow projecting them in front of you.

—I guess ... but now that you mention it ... You know what's weird? She's not four when I see her. She's my age. Or I guess maybe a little older, I'm not sure. But she's definitely not four.

—Then maybe you're sensing her spirit. And seeing her as she would have looked if she hadn't died. Unconsciously, I mean.

—You mean if I want to see her badly enough, I can make it happen? And I imagine her as my age or close to my age.

—Could be.

I thought about that. I guess it made sense. But how could I do that without knowing it? I wanted her to be real, not someone

I just imagined.

—Do you know how she died? Billy asked.

—I think she and my great-grandmother Iris died of pneumonia. I know Iris did, at least. They died around the same time. And something keeps coming back to me. It feels like a flashback that keeps repeating itself. We're at the river. Uncle Charles is handing Ave to Iris. And I'm almost certain we're participating in some kind of water ceremony.

—A water ceremony?

—Poppy says Iris' people perform water ceremonies during the fall when the leaves give their life force to the water. I have an image of Iris and Ave in the water. It must be one of my first memories. And unfortunately, the last of Ave and Iris. They must have caught cold from being in the water.

—And the cold turned into pneumonia.

—Doesn't that make sense?

—I suppose.

—It must have been cold that day because in my memory, I see snow flakes. Falling harder than they are now. I even see snow building on bare branches. Or at least that's what I think I remember. I get cold just thinking about it.

—Do you want to go back down?

—We probably should. Mama will …

Then something funny struck me. Snow in early October? Or, wait …

—It must have been September, I said aloud.

—What?

—Ave's gravestone says she died on October first. So the water ceremony must have been in September.

—And?

—Isn't that a little early for snow?

I tried to remember the earliest snows I'd experienced.

—I'll ask Doc or Poppy. They'll know if it snowed … if they'll talk about it.

—Just ask them about the snow. Don't mention Ave. Just ask them if it ever snows in September. If so, your memory makes sense. Otherwise …

—I guess I could be remembering the previous winter.

—The winter of 1921?

—Yeah, but I would have been an infant. Mama would have never let me out in the cold. Doc either. He's particular about babies. He tells mothers to be extra cautious with their newborns.

—Even for a special ceremony?

—I doubt he'd make an exception, even for a ceremony.

—Then maybe it can snow in September. An early cold snap could explain the bare branches. You want me to ask my dad to look it up?

—The weather?

—Sure. He's good at all kinds of research, has to be to write novels. So you wouldn't have to bother Doc and Poppy about something they might not want to talk about.

—That would be better.

Then it hit me what day it was. I was leaving on Monday.

—But it's the weekend, I said.

Billy looked disappointed.

—I'll ask Dad when I get home. Don't worry.

He pulled me back just before the bridge and kissed me on the lips.

—I'll see you tomorrow, he said and ran down the road.

I watched until he was out of sight.

Chick, Wink, Ipikam, Marina, and a royal entourage boarded canoes bound for the Temple of Ayla, deep within the Blue Ridge Mountains.

When they arrived, Chick knelt in the sparkling chamber and told his story: his flight from Opech, saving the people of Two Rivers, the flood that took him to Three Sisters, his heavenly wife and queen, losing his wife but gaining a daughter during another flood—only to lose her again, but happily finding her once more.

From the glittering rocks where she stood with the other sisters of the temple, Tesi listened. Swelling with tears, she said:

— This voice I hear …

Then her voice faltered, and she fainted, falling into the view of Chick and his party. Hearing her few words, Chick recognized the voice of his wife.

— My dead Tesi. And now … she is …

He knelt and took her into his arms.

— Come be buried again this time with me.

— That's it? Eva said. That's the end?

— Is there ever an end?

— Poppy, Eva said shaking her head. Don't tease. Is it the end of the story?

— I'm not teasing.

— But what happened to Tesi? Did she die? After all that? Or just faint.

— Does it matter?

That stopped her.

— I guess I'm not sure, she said quietly. I thought I was supposed to understand something.

— But you have, and that will help you make sense of life. Be intentional. Without intention you are immobile; your mind is immobile. Nothing important to you can be accomplished without your intention, understanding, and love.

— I have to want it?

— A fine way to put it, and that's the start. But just a start. Did Chick reach the temple on his own?

— He dreamed. And he had Wink and his entourage.

— And Ayla.

— He prayed to the goddess. But I don't really know any goddesses.

— Ah, not yet. But don't hurry your life. The point is Chick asked for help, for intervention. He asked for strength and power beyond himself.

Poppy pulled her to him, and they rocked gently on the porch. The evening stretched into darkness, mysterious unto itself. Rosa brought them a quilt. A few minutes later Doc held the door, and Rosa reappeared with two mugs of hot chocolate.

—Careful, she said. Hot. And look (*she nodded to the moon*), full tonight.

Poppy wondered how well he'd prepared Eva for what would come next. *You know you have*, Iris' voice came to him. *She has, is, and will be in good hands.*

Doc said:

When have I last looked on
The round green eyes and the long wavering bodies
Of the dark leopards of the moon?
For all their broomsticks and their tears,
Their angry tears, are gone
The holy centaurs of the hills are vanished.

Eva said:
—Beautiful but strange. Who?
—An Irishman. Yeats.

Then Doc stepped from the porch and disappeared into the darkness.

—What do you think he meant? Eva said.
—He might be doubting himself. He might have lost sight of the moon and other things that had been important to him.

She considered that.

—Could I be with Ave again if I really wanted to?
—There are ways.
—By wanting it enough? Or dreaming or asking for help?
—Those are all important pieces that will come together. You'll know when you are ready.
—How?
—How will you know?

He looked at the moon, searching for words. Then

Esperanza's voice chimed in: *Knowledge can come from anywhere. You may never know how or why.*

—Yes, he said aloud.

—Yes, what?

—I can tell you how it worked for me. For others here in the valley. But … I can't be sure if it will happen the same for you.

—What will happen?

—You know our family has gifts. To dream, to heal. Chick and his people are our ancestors. And Iris, your great-grandmother.

—Yes?

—But having a particular gift isn't necessary.

—Did Ave have a gift?

—Yes. Her gift was special. She's your uncle's daughter. And he is more special than you know.

—Charles?

—Charles knows how to control his gifts. Sometimes in ways I'd prefer he didn't … But we mustn't judge what people do with their gifts.

With two fingers, he tapped her nose, as if it were a miniature drum.

—You have desire and openness. You'll be fine. I am like you. We use our wills; we listen to our hearts. I've tried to teach you what I know, to develop your memory, to focus on the images, to recognize the symbols, the signs.

—Signs?

—Yes. My sign was a black iris.

—I don't think I've ever seen a black iris.

—Not yet.

—Will I?

—Iris was always their guardian. No one else knows where they grow. It might be down in those caverns. They get their power from another type of light than the sun. Iris said that when you're ready you'll find an iris.

—Did you find one?

—Well, more like it found me. She tucked one in my suit the day I got married. Said: *If you're not ready now, you never will be. Open your eyes. The waters are swift.*

—And then what?

—She pressed her palm to my chest and went to take her place for the ceremony.

—I mean after she gave you the iris. Could you do something special? Have visions? See into the future?

Poppy chuckled:

—I guess, Eva, my darling, it gave me that extra nudge we need sometimes. Faith in something beyond ourselves. But you're right. Afterward, my dreams and journeys were different, deeper.

Tears swelled in Eva's eyes.

—You're in good hands, Poppy said.

—But what if I don't find one … Poppy, I can't leave you.

Flint

We're riding down a long straight stretch of road. It feels strange—and good—to be in a car instead of a train. Doc and Mama discuss our route. We have to dip south before turning north again, and later Doc wants to make a stop. On the way to our new home. After a month of waiting and wishing we weren't going, I feel guilty to be excited about getting there. The world feels so new and bursting with color.

The sky ranges from pale baby blue to a bold true blue like the mill pond reflecting the sky to a dark purple blue near pillow-like clouds. Clusters of slate blue mountains rise solidly in the distant north and west. Butter yellow grasses whip in the wind, and wispy light blue-green-gray bushes—sage green like Rosa's kitchen curtains—shake and dance.

Rosa was stoking the wood stove when I hurried past her to the porch.

—Snow! I announced.

The early morning world glittered in a wafer-thin icing of snow. The eaves dripped, drip, drip. I inhaled the crisp almost metallic wet freshness mixed with wood smoke. Light flooded the valley. The wheel was turning, so I ran to the mill and went inside. Nathaniel came down the stairs from the loft.

—Hello there, missy. Fine morning ain't it?

—Yes, sir. Is Charles here?

—No, ma'am. Don't suppose I'll get much help from him for a while. You know how it goes.

—He's gonna go?

—Doesn't he always?

I ran back to the house and, catching my breath, asked Rosa:

—Is Charles going for the ginseng *now*?

—You know he is, child. First snow. It stuck, didn't it?

Each year Charles leaves right after the first snow. He's gone for a month or longer, and he comes back with a pack full of ginseng and other root herbs and plenty of wild stories.

Rosa had a double batch of corn biscuits baking, and they smelled marvelous, sweet and grainy. I was about to ask if I could help when Charles burst in and swung me into the air. Almost knocked over a chair.

—Eva May. You are getting as beautiful as your mother. I *swear*.

I giggled.

—Don't swear! Rosa'll wash your mouth out. Put me down. I'll help you get ready!

—I *am* ready.

—What?

—Sure. Started sticking 'bout midnight. Got Nathaniel set up in the mill. I'm packed. All I need now are these corn biscuits.

He kissed Rosa on the cheek and snatched a biscuit.

—Ah! he said, steam flying from his mouth.

—Patience, Rosa said.

I said:

—Why don't you wait until after we leave.

—And mess with tradition? he said with his mouth full of biscuit.

—But the plants will still be there. You can find them.

—Ah, yes. But they are ready now.

—But ...

I look out the car window. Leaves sprinkle down from the cottonwoods in a little town we're passing through. There are only a few buildings along the road. Farther off a cluster of houses suggests the heart of town. I wonder what people do here. I wonder if Charles' bags are full of ginseng yet. I wonder what Poppy and Rosa are doing right now. Is Poppy helping

Nathaniel? Is Rosa cleaning the house? Or cooking? What will they do with our rooms now that we're gone? Where's Kleela? Does she understand I didn't want to leave her?

I stood by the tulip poplar and watched Charles and Doc say goodbye at the bridge. Though I couldn't hear them, I could see Doc was doing most of the talking. Then they shook hands, and Charles called to me:
—It's time, little lady! Are you seeing me off?
—Yes.
—Then c'mon.
We climbed together. He was heading for my lookout as if he knew that's where I'd go.
—Are you sure I can't help carry something? I said.
—What? You think I'm not strong enough?
—No ... but I could still help a little ways.
—I told your mama, just up the hill. Then you'd be back down.
—But ...
He raised his eyebrow and gave me a look, which I thought meant *no arguing*. But when we got to the rocks, he said:
—C'mon.
—Really?
—Just to the river. Then after that you head straight back, you hear?
—I promise.
He walked quickly, and I hurried to keep up.
—Charles?
—Yep, he said without turning around.
—Do you know about black irises?
He laughed.
—Poppy been talking to you?
—Yeah. Well, do you know where we could find some?
—Sure.
—Really?
He stopped, turned and said:
—They'll find you.

—But couldn't we just look a little?

I was sure it was my time. I was with Charles, who was going out in search of plants, going down to the river … and I was trying to be as open to the idea as I could.

—Sure, he said. Look around.

—Here?

—Sure. Keep your eyes open. Ears too.

I slowed my pace and tried to pay attention. But it was hard to hear anything besides our trudging through the wet leaves and the melting snow dripping from the branches. After a while, Charles stopped and called back.

—They'll be wondering about you. Gotta pick it up. Or head back.

—I'm coming.

I trotted down the trail. Charles was filling his canteen at the seep.

—Here, he said, handing me the canteen.

I wanted to ask him about Ave and my memory at the river. But then I noticed his beads. Had they been there before? Like *hers*: small red and white beads, several strands close around his neck.

—Where did you get those beads?

He stood there fingering them.

—You never noticed them before?

I shook my head.

—Just kidding. I only wear 'em for collecting. It's tradition. For each root I dig up, one bead—and a prayer—return to the earth.

—Did Rosa teach you that?

He shook his head.

—Iris. C'mon, river's just down here.

He was down the trail again. I hurried to keep up with his long strides. I tried to find the right words, as we walked down the final stretch of path to the river.

—Uncle Charles?

—Yep.

—I … I just. Well … It's just that I won't see you for a long time, and I'd really like to know …

He turned at the riverbank.

—You wanna know about Ave and the river.

—How'd you know?

—We buried that, he said softly.

He sat on a log, and I stood in front of him, the river at my back.

—I just wondered if maybe …

—Silence is the glue that seals a secret. It has to be that way.

—But …

He shook his head and looked away. But he was beaming when he turned back.

—Don't worry, Eva, girl.

He patted the log, and I sat next to him.

—Sometimes giving away a secret muddies it. You'll understand in time.

He took out his pipe, filled it from his pouch, lit it, and slowly drew.

—Everything makes more sense when you figure it out yourself.

—But how can I learn anything else when I'm thousands of miles away?

He gave me a funny look and drew again.

—I heard Poppy telling you stories. You did listen, didn't you?

—You mean I'll see it in my mind?

—Something like that.

He laughed lightly and knocked the ashes out of his pipe. He pulled my head to his side and kissed my forehead. I smelled the burnt herbs.

—I've gotta go, he said.

He stood, so I did too.

—Which way do you go from here? I asked.

—Why straight across, of course.

—Charles. Oh, don't. Aren't you worried you'll catch cold? Can't you find a log to cross?

—Catch cold? In this water? What kind of cloudy head have

you got?

—But you'll be hiking around, and you could get sick. I know
you know your plants and all, but …

—Stop.

He grinned and set his pack down, then swooped me up like
he was going to toss me in the water.

—No, don't! I shrieked.

He put me back down.

—Lord, I know your father's *book* smart and all, but he forgot
to teach you some of the basics. Come here.

He squatted by the river, so I did too. Then he splashed me.

—How cold is that?

I was confused, not sure I'd felt the temperature. So I dipped
my fingers into the river. It was warm. I touched my wet fingers
to my cheek and asked him with my eyes.

—There's a hot vent in the mountain, he said, unlacing his
boots. Comes up into the river nearby. That's why we cross here.
I tell ya, girl. You've still got a few things to learn.

—I just never knew. No one told me.

He laughed and gave me a bear hug. He was half way across
the river before I could say goodbye. But by then the lump in
my throat kept me from saying anything. I could only giggle.
He looked so funny crossing in his undershorts, his pants and
boots slung across his shoulder. Before he was all the way across,
I finally called out:

—Charles!

—Yeah?

—Is this an early snow?

—Yeah, he laughed. It's early.

He shook his head and continued across.

—What's the earliest?

—What?

On the far bank, he dried himself off with his pants, then
pulled them back on and sat to lace his boots.

I called louder:

—What's the earliest snow?

He mumbled something I couldn't hear, and then something

caught his eye.

— Look! he called, nodding upstream.

A rainbow danced above the water in the rising mist, and for an instant I thought I saw something else, someone crossing in the mist.

When I looked back to Charles, he was gone.

— Charles? I called. Charles!

A raven flew overhead, and a thrush called.

— Charles!

The thrush sang again.

— Ave?

I looked upriver and saw a bird perched on a branch. No, there were two, a pair. They flew into the woods. And then the woods were silent, even the river.

Our road drops out of the mountains and stretches into long swaths of dry country. Doc says:

— In better times this would be grassland.

Just when I think there's not a soul for as far as I can see, a cluster of round huts appears in the distance, near a crossroads.

— That'll be our turn, Doc says.

When we reach the huts, he slows and turns onto a narrow dirt road.

— Look, I say. Huts ... or houses?

— Yes, Doc says. That's the style of the Navajo. Their houses are called *hogans.*

— But why are they round?

— It has to do with what they believe. I've heard them called *sacred spaces.*

— Will we be living in a round house in Django?

— Nope, afraid not. Most folks in Django prefer rectangular houses, just like in Virginia. But there were Indians in Virginia who lived in houses like these, the Cherokee, the Iroquois.

Different, but similar, you might say.

I thought about that.

It's a rough, lonely road, and we roll up the windows most of the way to keep out the dust. I trace the line of the horizon with my finger on the window. A few wisps of clouds, but the sky has become wide and vast, the bluest blue I've ever seen.

—Why does the sky look so big here? I ask.

—Because it is, Doc says with a wink I know well.

—But the sky's the same, I say. It's the same universe. It's just …

—Our perception. A wider view, like surveying the land from a high ridge or peak.

We hit a pot hole, and my head knocks against the window. *Ouch*, I sit back and close my eyes.

I visualize what I've just seen outside the car. The bushes are dry and scrubby, thin twigs of branches. They're marching into the distance, turning into a continuous carpet, a gray-brown sweep of a brushstroke. The road is narrow and straight. *The straight and narrow*, I hear Rosa say. The dust is a muted orange-brown. The sky is bright, stretching to the horizons.

When I think the wide flatness will never end, we dip down. *Ave, if you could see it, the bigness, the drop into the wide canyon.*

—Shouldn't be much longer, Doc says. Just up this wash.

A wash, I mean. It's not a steep narrow canyon. Not like your forested mountains. This canyon is … more like a bathtub. Do you use a bath tub? Or just the natural waters. How can I explain it. It's like the wideness of the sky on land. Like the Milky Way on earth: a big wide groove, carved into the land, a land that is like a skin stretched tight on a drum.

If I want it badly enough, can she hear me?

—Without intention, you are immobile, Poppy said. You must *will* it.

I imagine my desire is an eagle circling toward the sun.

Yes. The earth, Ave. I know you can hear me. I will it. Earth, tight like a drum. So big it makes you feel like an ant. I bet that's what the birds think of us when they see us bumping down the road. I can see for miles and miles. But not a single tree. Oh, yes, some of these shrubs are larger than others, but ...

Now where *was* the last tree? Somewhere this side of Santa Fe. But where?

—The ruins here at Chaco Canyon, Doc says, date back five to ten centuries ago, with extensive building. I know it's a little out of our way, but we should see them. You never know when we'll be back this way.

Doc stops the car beside a willow, with soft branches and narrow leaves, but smaller than what I'm used to back home where a willow can shade a yard. This one's just a shrub, not much taller than our car.

No shade, midday. A small stone building glares from the far side of a sandy dirt lot. Three horses eye us from a corral next to the building, their manes blowing in the wind.

—See? Doc laughs. Not that far off the beaten track.

—As if the train ride weren't long enough for you! Mama says, stepping out of the car and wiping her forehead with her handkerchief.

Her hair is wisping out of her braid, blowing like the horses' manes.

—My beautiful pioneer, he says and kisses her, a nice long kiss.

I look away, toward a wooden sign that says *University of New Mexico.* But I don't see any other buildings besides the one near the sign, just a few tents lined up.

—Call me what you will, Mama says, holding Doc's hand as we walk together toward the building.

A slender Navajo teenager in jeans and a red T-shirt walked from behind the building. He stopped at the fence and lifted one foot to the lower rung. One of the horses, a paint that Eva had been watching, nudged his arm. His gaze set on the family, the boy ran his fingers through the mane between the horses eyes.

Eva nudged Doc's arm and motioned toward the boy, who had climbed the fence, throwing his leg over to straddle the top, waiting. Doc called to him:

—Afternoon.

The boy nodded.

Doc said:

—We were told that someone from the New Mexico Field School might be willing to show us around the ruins.

The boy rubbed a smooth tan chin.

—Right now, he said, they're all at the sites. Won't be back till this evening. Who you looking for?

—Just someone who might be able to show us a few of the ruins. We're only passing through.

—Passing through?

—A side trip, Doc corrected himself.

—Well, the boy said, looking back at the three horses behind him, two paints and a roan. I could show you around, but ... you see, I'm supposed to be caring for the ponies.

—You know the ruins pretty well, then?

—Oh, yes. I know them as well as anyone. When Professor Hewett is working, I'm his right-hand man.

Doc nodded him on.

—I've heard so many of his talks I could tell you anything. I'm just not sure I have the time.

Doc rested his arm on the fence next to the boy and said:

—I think you'd make a fine guide, and we'd appreciate anything you could tell us about living out here. We've just come across the country from Virginia. We're relocating up the road in Colorado, on our way to Django now.

The boy nodded.

Doc continued:

—I bet the horses would be all right for an hour or so. Or we can wait while you take care of them. Now we'd compensate you for your time, of course.

The boy smiled.

—I suppose I could, he said and hopped off the fence.

Doc held out his hand.

—Doc Walton, he said, and this is my wife Leah and my daughter Eva.

—Jimmy, the boy said. Pleased to meet you.

He smiled at Eva, who blushed.

—You can follow me, he said.

As he walked to a gate in the corral, he pulled a bandana from his back pocket and tied it around his forehead, nodding to the paint and calling it with a short double cluck. The horse trotted to the open gate. Jimmy mounted him in a swift movement, reached down to latch the gate, and nodded to Doc.

—You follow in your car, Jimmy said. I'll get a head start.

He trotted his horse at a relaxed pace, down the dusty road edging the wide wash. At first, Eva couldn't see what the fuss was about or even where exactly they were heading. Then Jimmy stopped and walked his paint back to the Model A.

—You mind walking a little?

—We can walk! Eva said.

They left the road and started up a well-beaten path toward some high, sheer cliffs. A few minutes later they entered a world like nothing they'd ever experienced. Ahead of them, the stone ruins of an ancient civilization rose out of the sand.

Eva, walking beside Jimmy, wanted to ask questions. But she didn't know how to start. Ideas rolled about her mind like marbles. But nothing took hold. Now she could see other groups of ruins in the distance. Were they connected? How did they live out here? When were they built? Who lived here?

Then they were there, within a complex of stone walls, some barely breaking the ground surface, others closer to two stories high. Eva walked to a square window and waved through it to Doc and Leah.

—This way, Jimmy said. I think you'll want to see this.

He led them to the edge of a circular ruin, fifty feet across, sunken fifteen feet into the ground.

—You know what this is? Jimmy said, looking at Eva.

She thought about it, guessed:

—A place for storage? Grain storage. Like a silo?

Jimmy smiled.

—Yeah, maybe. Not a bad guess. But no one knows for sure. My people think these were sacred rooms. Scientists think so too. They learn a lot from talking to us, to the leaders of different tribes: Pueblo, Zuni, Navajo. The Hopi know more than the rest of us, but they don't like to talk much.

—Do you live in one of those circular … hogans? Eva asked.

—Of course, Jimmy said. Not far from here. But these ruins are different. They call these *great kivas*. There are other smaller kivas, but these large rooms, sunken into the ground, were special. See those stone circles on the floor of the room?

Eva nodded.

—They held huge tree trunks that supported the roof. Some of the scientists think the people hauled thousands of trees hundreds of miles to build Chaco. From as far away as Django. There's a place on the plateau where you can see the paths they made, roads leading north, south, east, west. They came and went in all directions. This was the center of the ancient people's religion.

—So, Eva said, do you know what they did in these rooms, these kivas?

—Secret rituals probably.

—Why secret?

Jimmy tilted his head and slid his hands into his back pockets.

—It's always been that way. Keeps them pure. There was probably a sipapu in the roof. See, the sipapu is this entrance, or passageway, for the souls to emerge from. And the souls, the people, go out on the path, to the center. And when they die, they come back. Out and in and back out again. Like the seasons.

—The sipapu, Eva said carefully. What is it exactly?

—Could be anything, a hole, pit, canyon even. A big round cave, it varies.

—And they go to the *center*?

—A middle place, a meeting ground, where all souls come together.

Eva thought about that and knelt beside the stone wall.

—May I? she asked, her hand hovering over the stones.

—Yeah, you're not gonna hurt anything.

Eva ran her palm over the smooth rectangular stones, each a unique shade of red, orange, tan, green, gray, purple, yellow. Jimmy squatted a few feet away, watching her. She looked into his dark eyes.

—You have beautiful eyes, she said, surprising herself the moment it slipped out of her mouth.

He tilted his head slightly and held her gaze until she looked away and said quickly:

—So, the souls go out and come back? It's kind of like the day after Halloween. In my grandmother's tradition, and my mother's, you go to your family graves, to remember.

—Yeah, Jimmy said, that's good. You have to remember; that's what my grandfather always says.

—Mine too, Eva said, standing.

—You wanna see some more? Jimmy said. This way.

He led them along a wall with square openings half way up the wall and circular openings a little higher.

—These were windows, he said, pointing to the square openings.

—And the rough openings higher up? Doc said.

—Rafters, Jimmy said. Logs brought from very far away.

They passed smaller circular rooms, everything clustered together but with a feeling of order.

—Think of all the people, Jimmy said. Many souls. See, it was a special place when it was active. But to many of us, it still is special, active. It's sacred. Grandfather says the ruins are the footprints of the ancestors.

—Must have been an extraordinary culture, Doc said. The masonry is incredible. That it survived so long. And *so* precise.

Doc knelt beside a wall and showed Leah how the smaller stones fit neatly between the larger ones.

—Yep, Jimmy said. Everything was intentional. That's why we have to respect them.

Jimmy pointed to a larger cluster of ruins about a quarter mile down the wash.

—See?

He leaned his head nearer to Eva's.

— More ruins? she said.

— Past that.

— Looks like wooden buildings?

Jimmy nodded.

— This guy came in and built a trading post right on top of Pueblo Bonito.

— Seems a little strange.

— The ancestors didn't like it. (*His voice became a whisper.*) Guy got murdered.

— Because of the trading post?

— Cursed, Jimmy said. Look around you (*he spread his arms wide, turning*). You can tell this place is sacred.

Eva and Jimmy ducked under a short, narrow doorway, entering a hallway that accessed a series of small rooms. Eva ran her hand along the stone walls, cool to the touch, and smooth. She stopped at each window to look out, wondering what people before her had seen.

— So, Eva said, how can you be *sure* he was cursed?

— Grandfather told me. It happened before I was born. But that wasn't all. A year later, the curse — 'cause this guy wasn't respecting the ruins — his little baby died too.

— All because of the buildings? But what'd the baby do?

— Nothing, Jimmy said. Her older sisters were out collecting flowers and gave the baby an iris. Baby ate it and died. Just like that. One year to the day after her father was killed.

— From an iris? Eva asked.

— Yeah, sure. But Grandfather says the baby didn't die from regular poisoning. Just faded away, stopped breathing. Could be because they didn't like what this guy was digging up. Folks around here say he was in it for profit. And some say he dug up secrets.

— Was he an archaeologist?

— Kind of. Some say he found caves with bones of people that had been murdered, people that came *before* these Chaco people. Bird people, feather people. They had feather blankets and baskets instead of deerskin robes and pottery.

—There were different people before these people who built the kivas and stone rooms?

—There's always someone who came before.

—Yeah, Eva said, thinking about Poppy, Chick, and the moon people. Why were the feather people murdered?

Jimmy laughed:

—Good question. But no one knows if they *were* or not. Or who they were. I've just heard people talk. Usually the scientists don't find bones that were crushed. They think most of the deaths were natural. But I don't know, I don't help out with grave sites, too many chindi, spirits. I'm just saying maybe this guy uncovered a secret he wasn't supposed to.

—That could be why he was cursed extra hard?

—Could be.

Eva and Jimmy reached a dead end, surrounded by shoulder-high walls.

—In and back out again, Jimmy said, smiling.

—Like the sipapu.

—Everything comes again.

Eva stopped at a window.

—I'm picturing the kiva.

—The great kiva?

—Yes, the first big one you showed us. There were windows in the wall, but you couldn't see out because it was below ground level, wasn't it?

—Yeah, I know what you mean. They weren't windows. Sometimes we find little pieces of pots or feathers or shells in there. And sometimes we find that kind of stuff buried in the walls.

—Intentionally buried?

—This one lady scientist thinks it's for forgetting.

—Forgetting? But why? If remembering is so important.

—In and out, Jimmy said. Back and forth, spring and fall, remember forget.

—Live and die?

Jimmy shrugged and led her back out of the corridor.

—Or, Eva said. Like stories and secrets. Real and imaginary.

Visible and invisible.

Jimmy smiled. They rounded a corner where Leah was leaning her back against Doc's chest as he pointed into the distance, talking softly.

—Boo! Eva said.

Leah turned and smiled sleepily in the sun.

—A private tour? Doc said, grinning. Now I've got a few more questions, Jimmy.

Doc led Jimmy by the shoulder, saying something about the cliffs and protection and water. Eva could hear Jimmy laughing.

—Mr. Walton, one at a time, please.

Leah said:

—It's getting late.

—Oh, but Mama, Eva said, looking out toward the distant ruins. There are so many more.

Red Bird

$\mathcal{S}$unday morning Billy was waiting at the bridge. I ran down to him, but before I could say hello, he said:

— No snow in September.

It took me a second.

— Right. How'd you find out?

— I told Dad it was important. And that you *had* to find out before you left. Do you want to go somewhere and talk?

We hurried up the hill toward the lookout. When we got there, Billy said:

— He thought it was an odd question. But he knows a professor in town. He has a fancy house and a pretty wife who served us tea and cookies. The professor showed us weather records and said it was highly unlikely that it'd snow in September here in Rockbridge County.

— You're sure.

— He was. I think that clinches it. You said it'd be unlikely for your parents to take you outside in the cold when you were a baby. So that rules out the winter of '21 to '22. And I think it's unlikely you'd remember anything when you were that young anyhow. According to the professor, there wasn't any snow in the fall of 1922 until *after* Ave died. Could it be someone else you're remembering? Someone you could have seen at two or three years old?

— If it's an actual memory.

— But, you said …

— It's just Poppy's story … I'm beginning to realize you can see memories that you never had or visions that maybe never happened. Or they happened, but you weren't there. How can you know? And how can I know if any of this is even possible?

—But you can trust Poppy.

—Yes. But I'd like to know it for myself.

—Maybe you do.

My eyes clouded. It had become confusing.

—There's another thing. I went with Charles yesterday, as far as the river. He left to collect ginseng. And the water was warm! He thought it was funny that I never knew that, but we never go down there.

—A hot springs!

—Yes. So Ave and Iris shouldn't have caught cold from being in warm water.

—So maybe your memory, or vision, doesn't connect to how they got pneumonia. If the water was warm.

—Yeah, Charles wasn't a bit phased. He dried off on the other side and disappeared just like that.

—What do you mean *disappeared*?

—It happened so fast. He pointed upriver, to a rainbow above the water. I looked. It was beautiful. When I turned back he was gone.

—Without saying goodbye?

—It was hard to hear across the water.

Billy looked at his hands, then down toward the farm. I tried to see what he saw. He was new here. I had lived on the farm all my life. I tried to imagine it without me. Aunt Katie was sitting on her glider. She held her shawl at her throat. She swung back and forth. No effort to it. She looked out across her flower beds, the way she always does. But in my dream I'd been there.

—Where are you? Billy said.

—Sorry.

—Maybe we shouldn't think about it?

—About Ave? I said.

—No, that's fine. You know …

Then he put his arm around me.

—You know, your mom can't really see us up here.

I wasn't sure what he meant, but when he leaned toward me

I got the picture.

—Billy Morgan!

I pushed him away.

—Just kidding, he said.

I hopped down from the rocks. He walked behind me when the trail narrowed, and I regretted having pushed him away. I replayed how his arm felt around my shoulder. Testing myself. After today I'd only be able to imagine it. *Yes, I could feel it.*

Can I still feel it? I feel silly for what I said to Jimmy, about his eyes. *I didn't mean it, Billy. I just want you.* I close my eyes and rest my head against the seat. The road is smooth now, and Doc says it shouldn't be much longer. The sun is setting. I relax my shoulders and feel Billy's arm wrap around them.

Comforted, I took a deep breath and returned to Ave. I thought about the dates on the gravestones and my memory, or vision, which might be a better way to explain it since I wasn't even sure it was my own memory.

I turned back toward Billy and said:

—So how do you tell if a memory is really yours? If you think you remember something, how do you know you're not just creating that image out of thin air? Or that the image wasn't from someone else's memory?

—Good question. If someone can confirm the memory? If they remember it too? Then two heads are better than one, right?

A squirrel scurried up a tree. I remembered I should be looking for the irises. I wanted to be ready. I felt ready. But how do you know? For sure.

—What were you saying? I said.

—If a second person can confirm the memory.

—Oh, sure. Unless they're wrong too.

—But how can both people be wrong?

I looked around, scanning the undergrowth. It had to be my time, the irises must be right under my nose.

—But if every detail were the same, Billy said.

—Every detail? Well ... how many details would it take? And

what if most of the details were the same, but a few were different? (*That's where the mayapples bloom. And there's a spiderwort.*) And if you don't have a memory of a particular time, does that mean it never happened?

When do irises usually bloom?

—We can't remember everything, can we?

—What? You think we run out of brain cells? We block some things out, but we could remember everything if we wanted to. Doc says we get clogged up, and that's one way of looking at disease. When we're out of balance, with too much of something or not enough of another, our chemicals get confused and send the wrong messages.

Am I diseased?

And what about what Jimmy said about that baby? An innocent baby. Did the iris really poison her?

—How does that relate? Billy said.

—Oh, I just mean … it's confusing. Where do dreams come from? Where do memories come from? Why do we have some and not others? I get so turned around I forget what I'm looking for.

—Ave?

—Yeah, like Ave. Maybe … maybe the gravestone is wrong.

—Why would they make a mistake on a gravestone?

—Maybe it wasn't a mistake.

—Why would they lie about when someone died?

I remembered Edmund. *Wasn't he saying something about crimes?*

—Maybe, I said, they were covering up something.

—Something that Ave would be involved in?

—Or Iris. Maybe she was accused of a crime. I don't know, a murder or something. And then she died. But they moved the dates back to show she couldn't have been involved in the crime.

—Couldn't they have just stood trial? Why would they accuse an old woman—no offense, but she'd have been pretty old, right? And if she were dead, then would it really matter anyhow? To save her reputation, I guess?

—Iris was different. Yeah, she'd have been older, but … (*What was it that Edmund had said about her? Or was it Doc? She was a better healer. She could disappear.*) Maybe Edmund didn't like it that she was different. Maybe he thought she killed someone through black magic.

—In the twentieth century?

I wonder. Maybe the baby just disappeared?

I could hear the desperateness in my voice. I wanted to understand. I said:

—There's *got* to be some kind of cover-up going on.

—Should I see if my dad can check the courthouse records?

—Well … there was something that Chick said yesterday.

—Chick?

—Did I say that? I meant Charles. (*I laughed uneasily.*) Charles said silence is the best seal. If they wanted me to know about it, they'd have told me.

Silence and stories, I remember Jimmy saying. Or did I say that? *In and out, spring and fall*, I think I remember him saying. *Remember forget.* No.

—Maybe it would be *bad* to uncover something, I suggested slowly. Maybe it's safer the way it is.

I looked back to see if Billy had heard me. He had been looking down, then caught my eye, said:

—I guess that makes sense. But it's hard to leave a mystery unsolved once you know about it.

—Unless there are multiple solutions.

—This is starting to sound like the Visible and Invisible Universe.

—Could be.

When we got to the seep there were icicles.

—Ice, Billy. Look.

He squatted and ran his finger over one, then said:

—But it's got to be above freezing.

—Cold air leftover from last night.

I squatted beside him.

—You can drink it. It's good water.

He cupped his hands under the trickle and sipped.

—This is good. How come you never brought me here before?

I shrugged.

—I've only been here a couple of times, just this fall. And we're supposed to stay in sight of the farm.

—What are they gonna do? Ground you? Forbid you from seeing me?

—They can't do that.

He reached for my hands and pulled me to him and kissed me on the lips. And he kept kissing me. *It felt so good.* He held me to him.

I should have paid more attention so I'd remember it better. But thinking about it now, I feel dizzy, as if my insides have turned to jelly. My body remembers it even if I'm not certain of the details. So sweet. *He* was so sweet.

—I won't let you go, he said. I'll kidnap you. I'll hide you.

—OK, I said, grinning. Where?

—You ... wanna go back, don't you.

I hesitated, then said what he knew I'd say:

—I have to.

But he stood between me and the path back to the farm.

—Billy?

—Not yet. I'm not ready.

I smiled, took a deep breath, and made a break, scrambling up through the rocks and saplings.

—Catch me!

He was right behind me in no time.

—Gotcha, he said and held on to me.

We tumbled into the wet leaves.

—Rosa'll have dinner on, I said. They'll look for us if we're not back soon.

He sat behind me now, wrapping his arms around me.

—I know, he said and rested his head on my shoulder.

—That must be it, Mama says.

There's a light on over the porch. As we turn in, I see a small woman with long black hair sitting on the porch steps. Or maybe it's just the dimming light of twilight.

Doc pulls the parking brake. The woman stands, and a breeze blows her white cotton dress. She pulls a red and purple shawl around her, and I can see her arms are darkly tanned. She smooths a loose strand of hair back behind her ear and walks toward the car.

—*Bienvenidos*, she says as we step out. Welcome.

—You must be Esperanza Domingo-Rodriguez, Doc says.

—Ah, you are a smart man, Doc Walton. I am very glad to see you again.

—Again?

—Yes, I have pictured you. You are as handsome as I thought. And (*she turned to Mama*) you must be the beautiful Leah.

She embraces Mama, kisses her cheeks.

—And Eva, she says, hugging me and holding me close for several seconds. You are exactly as I imagined.

Esperanza Domingo-Rodriguez isn't much taller than I am.

—I'm sorry if we kept you, Doc says.

—Oh, it's no problem. I was in the area.

—Do you live in the neighborhood? Mama says.

—Oh, no. Not me. Me and my son, we live near Mancos. But you know, I come here to town to check on my people. I have my hands full, Doc. We are all very glad you're here.

—We'll have to get started right away.

—Yes. You see that can be your office, she says pointing to a smaller building attached to the main house via a covered walkway.

—Can we go in? I ask.

—It's your home, she says. Not much inside right now. But we'll help you find everything you need.

The rooms are smaller than the ones in Virginia. This house is only one story, and it's made of smooth stone. Adobe, Doc says. It's lovely and cool inside. Esperanza is right; there's not much furniture yet, but I see a room that I bet will be mine.

—Can I go explore? I ask Mama when she comes in and sees me admiring my room.

—It's getting dark.

—It just looks that way from inside, I say. There's still time.

Mama puts her hands on her hips and smiles, barely.

—Can I trust you to stay in sight this time?

—Mama, I'm twelve years old. We were right behind the rocks; you just couldn't see us.

—Well, I certainly do not like the idea of you hiding behind rocks. Especially with older boys. And this is a new place.

She walks me out to the back porch and points up the hill of sagebrush.

—I don't want you going into *any* woods. Please stay out in the open where we can see you.

—I will.

—And be back in half an hour.

—Mama.

—No longer. Got it?

—I promise. I'll be back by supper.

—Esperanza Domingo-Rodriguez has brought a very nice platter of enchiladas. I don't want the first person we meet to have to come looking for you.

—Mama, please! I just want to go find a quiet spot and write in my journal.

I show her my journal and pencil. She kisses my forehead and shakes her head as she turns to go. But Esperanza is there in the doorway.

—Ah, I see Eva is ready to know the land, she says.

—Is there anything out there she should watch out for?

—Oh, dear! she says and squeezes Mama's shoulder. This child? Do not fear. She will be just fine. I know.

Mama looks back up the hill hesitantly.

—I go with her, Esperanza says. We'll have a little walk.

And to me:

—Is that an OK idea?

We walk through the garden gate.

—You smell the sage? she says. It rained this afternoon.

I inhale deeply.

—Yes, she says. You'll learn to *love* that smell.

We climb slowly to where the smaller pines start to meet the sagebrush.

—Hear that? she says.

I listen, but I don't hear anything. Then I do, a flute. Or no, not quite.

—It sounds familiar, I say. Like a thrush, but …

—Meadowlark. Usually you hear them more in the spring, but this one is happy about something.

The pines start to close in around us, but they're shorter than the pines in Virginia. I point to one of the sword-leaved pincushion plants.

—Yucca, right? We saw these on the train.

—Yeah, she says and kneels beside it. Very helpful plant. You can make all sorts of twine and cord, sandals. And the root (*she pats the ground like it's a baby's head*) will make your hair long and shiny. Suds up, you'd like it. I'll show you, soon.

She takes my hand as she stands. And she points to another plant just up the slope.

—You know this one? she says and picks a feathery green leaf.

—It looks like a fern. But it's not, I add quickly.

I bring it to my nose.

—Minty.

—Well, you remember that one. Good for your periods.

—My …? Oh, I haven't started yet.

—No? Oh, well, soon enough. Soon enough.

We sit on a fallen log, the wood worn smooth but full of

woodpecker holes.

—You'll like it here, she says.

—It's so different. I'm sure it's fine, but … I really didn't want to leave Virginia. (*I look at her apologetically.*) I'm sorry. I know Doc'll help a lot of people. It's just leaving my family …

—But not so far away for you, young woman.

I'm not sure what to say to that.

—Your Poppy has taught you, yes? When you need to go back home, just take the steps, practice your journeys.

—Walk through the days. Yes, I was about to finish my journal. But, how do you know Poppy?

—Come, come. Did you ever wonder how Poppy could see all this about to happen and *know* it was right? Do you think instinct is simply acquired with age? He practiced. All his life. And his mother is a great teacher. Dear, when you need to see him, when you need to escape, when you need to be in another place, you can be there. He taught you to journey, yes? Here, hold my hand. I'll walk you through one of mine.

She takes my hand in both of hers and looks around us.

—Let's see. Is this a good place?

She breathes deeply, and I follow.

—Yeah, she says. I think this will do. Now close your eyes.

I close my eyes. I hear the meadowlark sing.

—First, let yourself see a big hole in the earth. An entrance to the underworld.

—The underworld? I say and open my eyes.

Hers are still closed.

—Let's call it the *inner* world then. And close your eyes. It helps to block out distractions.

I close my eyes. How did she know?

—Do you see it? she says.

—Any kind of hole?

—A cave, a tunnel, a pit …

—A cavern?

—Sure, OK.

I see one of the caverns back in Virginia. Dripping with sparkling formations. I hear water flowing in the distance.

—OK, she says. You're at the entrance?

—Yes.

—What's next? What do you see?

—I see shimmering rocks.

This feels good. Like playing one of my games with Poppy or Doc or Billy. Maybe I'll be able to see Billy or Ave.

—OK, that's good, she says. You see shining rocks. You see the entrance. How large?

—Twice my height.

—OK, you see a large entrance, then shining rocks. Rocks are good, yes. They know. Then what?

—It gets kind of dark.

—Do you see an arch?

I try to see an arch.

—Maybe.

—Good, good. Go through it. Entrance, rocks, arch.

I try to see myself walking under the arch.

—Don't see yourself, she says. *See.* You are *there*, what do *you* see?

I hear her get up and stand behind me.

—Here, she says and massages my shoulders. Relax. That's good, yes.

—I … I think I see a larger opening. It's lighter.

—Yes, and then what.

My mind pops to Rosa's kitchen. She's cooking tomatoes.

—I see our kitchen! I say, eyes still closed. I can smell the tomatoes. And, and … (*I look around.*) I see my Grandma Rosa, but I don't see Poppy. (*I look harder. I look outside.*) He must be down at the mill.

I open my eyes.

—But it's not the same.

—It's a good start, she says. Come. Your father will have gotten the stove going by now.

—But I was getting somewhere.

—Oh, you need to relax. There are many places. You'll see. You'll learn.

—But I'm ready, now.

—Patience, yes? she laughs. Come. Good enchiladas are waiting. And my roasted blood turnips, blackest skinned beet around. And oh so tender. You'll love 'em.

Flower

I wake early with the sun rising over the hill I see from my bedroom window. So that's east, or a little south of east.

Mama is grinding coffee when I come into the kitchen.

— You're an early bird, she says.

— I'm going to the edge of the woods, to the piñons where Esperanza took me.

Mama looks out the window, then at me and sees my coat in my arm.

— Bundle up. And you know the rule.

— I'm twelve years old, Mama.

— Stay in sight. Be back in half an hour. Esperanza Domingo-Rodriguez brought us tortillas for breakfast, and Doc went with her to meet a patient. We'll have eggs as soon as they're back.

— Don't worry so much, I say and hug her. Your new piano's coming this morning. You probably won't even realize I'm gone.

Then Mamas stops. Her eyes widen, and she listens, then starts untying her apron.

— That could be it coming now, she says and squeezes me. Have fun. And be careful!

I climb through the sagebrush. The early morning air is cool, fresh. Doc said the Animas river is on the other side of the ridge, and that he'll explore it with me soon. But first I've *got* to finish my journal. You'd think I'd have had time enough on the train to recall twenty days accurately. But I still have a day to go.

I watch a big bird soar low barely above the sagebrush. It might be a hawk, but it's strange for a hawk, not like the red-tails in Virginia that soar high in the sky. And it has a white patch on its back near its tail feathers. I turn, my head to the sky, to watch it change course and—Ugh! I trip and—Ouch, I catch my fall on a … on a yucca. Their leaves are like daggers! A drop of blood beads on my finger. That's all, but it hurts like a hurricane. I shake out my hand and continue up to the log. I press my hand on its cool, smooth surface. I lower my cheek to it and listen.

A raven calls, then a second, and both birds appear. They alight together on an old wooden arch down the slope. One makes a low croaking sound and looks toward me. The other turns toward me as well, then both jump back into the sky and fly away. I look down into the valley and think about Virginia, home. My lookout there was higher, but I can see farther from here. It seems like a long time ago when we left Virginia.

I focus on the days. Turtle through Flower. And the days start over again.

That morning was cool like *this* one.

—You will do as I asked you? Poppy said, looking deep into her eyes, his hands holding her shoulders square.

—Every day, she said. I promise.

They stood by the creek, near where the run diverted water away to the mill. Poppy put his arm around her, and they walked slowly along the creek toward the car. Kleela walked a dozen yards in front.

—Yes, I'm sure you will. Turtle, whirlwind, hearth, dragon.

—Serpent, twins, deer, rabbit, she continued.

—The river, he said, stopping and nodding out across the valley.

—Wolf. Raccoon, rattlesnake tooth, reed, panther, eagle, owl.

—Heron. Flint.

—Red bird.

—And today? he said.

—Flower. And tomorrow it's turtle again.

—Yes, it starts anew. *See* each day. *See* each place. Smell it, hear it. Feel it, trust it. Let it take you where it wants to. Hear the rhythms of the landscapes in your dreams. Listen to your heartbeat. Call on those you trust for assistance. Remember Chick's long journey home to his family.

—And *want* it deep down in my bones.

—Intent. Yes, my darling. You must desire it.

—If I want to see you. If I really want to see you and not just remember you.

—It is the intent to receive what the spirits around you have to offer. If they have a vision of me to offer, then yes, you will see me.

Poppy and Eva watched as Doc walked up the slope from the car to meet them.

—We're all set, he said.

Then he and Poppy embraced, long and strong, and then stepped back from each other.

—We'll be waiting at the car when you're ready, Doc said to Eva, brushing her cheek. But the train won't wait for us.

At the car, Rosa kissed her son and embraced Leah. She didn't bother to hold back her tears. Katie stood with them, shaking her head.

—I just don't understand it. But God bless you and watch over you. You be back soon, now.

Eva knelt to hug Kleela one last time and rose, her face wet with licks. Eva's tears seeped onto Rosa's warm shoulder. She forced a brave smile as she said goodbye to Poppy. She watched them out the back window until the car rounded the first curve. And still, she saw them waving to her.

I set my journal down and breathe deeply. I brush the tears from my cheeks and hear a whisper of Mama playing her new piano. Her notes mix with new bird songs I want to learn. I close my eyes and listen, and breathe. In ... as deeply as possible. All the way. Then out, slowly ... as slow as possible, until every wisp of air is out. I feel Poppy's hands on my shoulders, and a heaviness lifts as Mama's playing and the bird songs come together in my mind ... a flute.

I picture the cavern I saw with Esperanza. I place my hands on the cold ground beside me. The earth is hard, rough, and it takes a while, but then I see the entrance. The rocks are glowing and ... I feel so light, as if I'm falling ...

Poppy, I'm here. Help me see, Poppy, Iris, Ave. I'm here.
I see the days.

> *Turtle* — The news I didn't want to hear
> *Whirlwind* — Looking for something or lost
> *Hearth* — Telling Billy
> *Dragon* — Stirring, stirring
> *Serpent* — Pleas
> *Twins* — E-o-ah she called
> *Deer* — The haunted cabin of course it was
> *Rabbit* — Annabel Lee
> *The River* — The river
> *Wolf* — Kleela
> *Raccoon* — Oh that kiss
> *Rattlesnake Tooth* — Lamont, I hope you are well
> *Reed* — October 1, 1922, no ...
> *Panther* — The mirror
> *Eagle* — Lights to remember
> *Owl* — Dreaming, dreaming
> *Heron* — Snow?
> *Flint* — Thrushes fly
> *Red Bird* — Don't leave me
> *Flower* — I'll be seeing you

Flower — Seeing you. Turtle, flower, and back to Turtle. The days come round again. Like the petals of an aster.

bundled together
count them before
they fall

each one
that lingers
becomes

the one
waiting
for the sun

The flute calls me. The entrance, the rocks, the arch is wide. I drop down, not afraid this time. I land and kneel on a mossy pad. The rocks glow violet, blue, white. I feel the water, warm when I press my fingers into the moss.

I hear laughter. Focus. The room is large, bright. Dripping. Laughter Echoes. Dripping all around. And what is that, a flower?

—Ah, come now, come now, the voice says and laughs farther away.

The flute is louder. My head spins.

—Ah, yes, now. You are here.

A little brown man appears.

—Come now. That's a good girl. This is the way.

He skips away. I follow. Down the large tunnel—or is it a hall?—lit with candles. Lots of candles. Who tends them? The walls are painted with flowers and strange creatures, and …

—Come now, dear. Don't be late. It's time.

He skips off laughing. At me? He sounds like many voices together.

I run after him and collide into … a woman.

—I'm so sorry, I say.

She's taller than I am and beautiful. Her long blond hair flows around her ivory cotton dress. Her lips look as soft and red as rose petals. Her skin, smooth and fair.

—I know you, she says, studying my face. You're Eva. I've

always wanted to meet you, dear. Poppy said we should be expecting you to visit.

—But where am I?

—Here, she says, handing me a lily of the valley.

It smells sweet and earthy. Like the farm. Then I hear something, and the row of bell-like flowers tremble.

—Listen, she says.

I hear distant bells. The sound of water on icy light.

—They're happy, I say.

—Lilies return happiness. Iris says that's what hooked Charles. He found happiness in the face of war.

—What? Are you talking about …?

—I'm taking too long. You're here to see something.

—But I thought you were …?

—Death is a new beginning. Let's walk. (*She takes my hand.*) Easy now.

We walk down a steep stairway to an underground river and stop at the edge. It's too wide to leap across, and there's no bridge.

I look into a pool and see myself. Then I feel her warm body against my back, and I look for her reflection. But a ripple spreads across the water.

—This way, she says.

She takes my hand, and we walk upstream to where she eases into the water. Her dress flows around her.

—Look, she points downstream. Can you see it?

I kneel and balance myself with one hand pressed against the wall.

—Listen, she says.

I hear water. And somewhere in the distance a flute. Or Mama's piano? And high notes, *E-o-ah*, Eva.

—Is it Ave?

I look around. But she's gone, or was never there, and a small lily of the valley floats by. As I watch the flower ride out of sight, I see something in the distance … the water flowing under the bridge at the farm. I squint.

Yes. I see the farm. I can smell it, the dry grasses, the wet leaves, the wood smoke. And the wheel turns round and round. There it is. And Nathaniel. He's resting his banjo under the window and going inside the mill.

—Nathaniel? I call hesitantly.

But he's inside.

—Eva. My darling.

I look behind me. Poppy is coming down from the barn.

—You made it.

—But how can I be here?

—You wanted it, didn't you?

—What does this mean?

He nods.

—Ah, that is a fine question.

We sit together. He's wearing his thick leather work gloves. The wind is blowing from the southwest.

—Did you enjoy your journey?

—But I'm right back here, Poppy.

I press my hand into his chest to see if he is real.

—I came through a cave. And there was this woman … And yesterday Esperanza helped me see the entrance. But do you mean the train? It feels like we were on it forever. But no time passed at all. Because we're right here. Was I dreaming? Is Billy here? Where's Rosa? Can I see Ave?

He looks into my eyes.

—Am I dreaming? I say.

But he doesn't answer me; he only looks toward the road and turns his head to the side.

—Hear that? he says, easing up to stand. My, it's getting cold.

I listen. I hear Mama's piano. And there's someone laughing again, couldn't be just one, a whole bundle of 'em.

—Is someone laughing?

—No, listen. Hear the wheel turning? Here, Eva.

—I … Oh yes, I hear the wheel. And … is there a car?

I see it creep around the bend. A big, dark black new model. *Edmund*, I think.

—Should I go? I ask, my heart racing.

—Yes, Eva. Go now. Quickly. (*He kisses my forehead.*) You know the way.

He gives me a pat as I turn to run back up the hill, but I immediately crash into the cavern wall. And my foot slips back into the river. My head aches, and there's laughter again. I close my eyes and hold my head. I see my finger: blood.

Then someone taps my shoulder. Tap, tap.

—Time to go. Time to go. Yep, yep. Oh, dear. Joe is waiting. You must be more careful. From now on.

He giggles and straightens my shoulders so they rest against the wall. But I lean over on my side; my head is spinning. I'm going to cry. And oh, the cackling, it hurts my ears. Are they laughing at me? But it makes me want to laugh too.

He tries to straighten me again.

—No, I say.

—Eva, he insists.

His voice is deeper now. His hands stronger. I look up and shriek.

—Eva. It's OK.

But … don't I know you?

—Joe? I say and shake my head. My brain rattles around like a bowl of black walnuts.

But I don't know him. Is this déjà vu?

—Yes, it's me, he says. How did you know?

I can see down to the house, and I know exactly where we are. I shake my head, but it doesn't rattle this time. He offers his hand to help me up. He's tall and slender, older than Billy but younger than Charles. His arms are smooth, muscular. And he's wearing odd padded leather boots. With his long dark hair tied back, he reminds me of Poppy.

—This feels like déjà vu, he says. I've been looking for you all day. I can't believe you were right here all this time. Did you find your way to the river and back? I imagined finding you so many times. That must be why it feels like I've been here before.

We walk down the hill together, and I'm not sure what to say. Then I remember.

—Wait.

193

I turn to go up the hill.

—I'll be right back.

My journal is still at the log. I reach to grab it, but there's a feather on top. Reddish brown, it blends with the leather. I pick it up and hold it to the light, which is … I must be turned around, because I thought that was west. I look back to where I thought I saw it rise. Then I look back to the feather and roll the shaft between my fingers. I place it carefully at my last entry, keeping my place. And I trot back down to the man, Joe, watching for rocks as I go.

Mama met us at the garden gate.

—Where in the *world* have you been?

She wipes her brow then pulls me tight to her chest.

—What … do you mean? I say, enveloped in her bosom.

I pull back and look around the garden, then back up the hill.

—Eva May. You are not to go wandering off like this. Not now, not right away. Honey, we've got to get adjusted. There are all sorts of things out here you don't know about and …

Joe says:

—She was safe enough up there, but better not to fall asleep when you're new to a place.

Mama says to Joe:

—Thank you so much for finding her.

—If she wanders off again, call me. But I expect she's learned her lesson, right?

He looks at me, and I don't know what to say. Then he walks to his horse and mounts, as Doc drives up. Joe waits until Doc gets out, and they shake hands. Joe rides off, and Doc walks around the side of the house to where Mama and I stand together.

—Eva, and Leah, the beautiful mother of my daring child. *Gifted*, I might add.

He pulls us to him and kisses Mama's cheeks. Mama starts to say something, but Doc stops her and says to me:

—Gifted simply to try. To work hard and believe. To believe what feels true but nothing more. Isn't that right?

—Sure.

I'm relieved. I don't think I'm going to be punished. Then Doc says:

—But you need to work on your perception of time.

—OK, but first how about those tortillas Miss Esperanza brought for breakfast.

—Try supper, Mama says.

—Supper?

—You've been out all day. I'm not surprised you're hungry.

I laugh, or try to, as we walk inside. The kitchen smells of earthy corn and tomatoes. I'm not sure what they're talking about, but I am famished.

Mama says:

—I learned Southern cooking, and I'll learn Southwestern cooking too. Esperanza showed me how they make tamales. She brought some of her special sauce.

—Is she gone?

—Eva May, Mama says. What shall we do with you?

Doc says:

—Esperanza said she'd be fine. Said she showed her a trail that leads out from here.

—Yes, but Eva doesn't know this place yet.

Doc just nods and says:

—By the way this kitchen smells, I'd guess you've both adjusted to your first day here. Your cooking smells right fine. And Eva's come home after her first adventure.

—I guess maybe I fell asleep? I say.

—It has been a long trip, Mama says. Oh, I almost forgot.

She leaves the room and returns with an envelope.

—The postman stopped by. This came for you.

I read the postmark: Lexington, Virginia.

Dear Eva,

I found this after you left. We have some like it back home, so I thought of you. You're what made me feel at home here. I couldn't believe it was in bloom this late in the year.

I found it up past the lookout. Remember when I surprised you up there that day? I relive that day every day. It feels more and more real instead of farther and farther away. I'll go again and practice our memory journeys. You're my Annabel Lee. Gone, but always close to my heart. I'll go there, and I'll hear the birds you taught me to hear. I'll see what you taught me to see. I'll see you.

And know what else? When I replay my days with you, I see more and more. Just like you told me I would.

Your friend,
Billy

Three folded pieces of paper are tucked into his letter. I sit on the piano bench and open them one by one.

Big orange pumpkins
round the sky
I pull a shawl around her
as we enter a cavern
an asterisk of light flashes by

I touch cold rock
and jump back
finding something warm—
her hand
although I can't see her

FLOWER

I stare into
a jeweled place
into Ice's eyes
I hear the ticking of a clock
in my dream.

She called it
Turtle
pleased

to be
one
with you

taking
our time
by the elm

to wager
how tall
we are

imagining
ourselves
stacked

on top of
each other
to estimate

FALL OF '33

you remind
me you are
one inch taller

so I straighten
my trunk
to see

eye to eye
limb to limb
we climb

I see
your legs
I dare

not turn away
you are right
again

it *is* taller
like you
than me

your skirt flies
up as you
jump down

you win
and I win
I long

to stretch
my arms
around you

FLOWER

instead
I dance
in a dream

with you
and all the time
in our world.

    I unfold the third, and a tiny, deep indigo iris slips into the palm of my hand.

Epilogue

Poppy watched the car drive up the lane toward the house. Edmund was the only one in town he knew with a Model B. He said to Rosa:

—I'll make sure he doesn't go looking for Charles. I'll convince him he's gone south, not north …

But as it got closer, he saw two figures in the car.

Will first, then the boy, got out. Will watched the boy race away from the road and up the hill where he turned to wave once, then kept on running.

Although Billy knew better, he hoped Eva would be high on the hill waiting for him. When he reached their lookout, he leaned against the rocks, keeping his feet firmly planted on the earth, as if drawing an imaginary line between the rest of the world and his secret world with Eva.

Poppy removed his work gloves and walked toward the car. The men shook hands.

—Mr. Walton, Will said.

—Yes, Mr. Morgan. It's good to see you. Billy said you had some questions you'd like to ask me.

—I appreciate you sending word back that you'd be willing to oblige me.

—I'm pleased to meet with you, Mr. Morgan.

—Call me Will.

—I will …

—I'd like to learn about some of your people's ways.

Poppy chuckled:

—Most people prefer to imagine the future not the past.

—You'd think the past would be easier.

—It is more predictable, Poppy said, if you can remember it.

Then Poppy nodded toward the hill across from the farm and said:

—Billy's a fine young man.

Will said:

—Yes, he is. Should I call him back? He's getting pretty determined these days.

—No need. He'll be fine.

The chill of the early November day had been driven off by the sun. The breeze had an edge, though not yet the burden it would become in winter in the hilly farm country. Will wore a crisp white shirt, sleeves rolled to his elbows, and a black leather vest. He looked past the barn and up toward the woods high behind it.

—You have a nice place here.

—Thank you … So how can I help you?

—I'm a writer, or trying to be. I'm also teaching a couple of courses at the college.

—You're a professor?

—Well, not really. Just an instructor. But if I can write a good book or two, perhaps I'll become a professor one day. And that's what I'd like to talk with you about. Not about becoming a professor, I mean. But writing …

Poppy laughed softly at that. And Will looked at him kindly as they sat on the porch steps. Will's eyes sparkled blue. A breeze that spun up from the road played with his thin sandy hair. But he ran his fingers back through it and straightened it down. He drew his notebook out of his vest pocket and continued:

—I understand from some of the folks around here that you're an expert on some … arts, that you learned from your ancestors.

—Which folks say that? Poppy asked, curious now that someone was talking about him.

—Well, Mr. Walton, you got me there. Actually, the folks I refer to are my son Billy and your granddaughter Eva.

—You know my granddaughter well?

—Well sir, not exactly. But my son, as you know, has spent a good deal of time with Eva. And I take it from the way he speaks of her, they thought—think—quite well of each other. And to try to get myself out of this conversational bind I've talked myself into, let me say clearly that the information I have about your knowledge of some ancient arts comes entirely from Billy.

—So what kind of arts did Billy tell you about?

—To be honest, sir, I'm not at all clear about what he told me. He said Eva told him on several occasions that you have been teaching her *secrets* about memory, stories that were passed down to you long ago. That you were passing them along to Eva.

—What else did Billy say?

—Not too much, really. It was clear from what little he said that Eva considered these stories very special, and … And maybe I should emphasize that Billy thinks he's sworn to secrecy, even from his father. That's why *he* suggested I come here. You see, I admit I've been having what's called *writer's block*.

—So you're requesting information from me to help you get over your writer's block. Is that about right?

Will turned away to compose himself. He straightened his strong square chin and took a deep breath. He believed he'd said too much. But we say what we need to say or feel we have to say. And when you're in a tight spot, and the outcome matters to you, there's no way out except to try to say what you need to say. When he turned back, he was ready.

—I know you're a busy man. I can't pay you much for talking to me. But I'll introduce you in my book and give you full credit for everything you're willing to tell me.

—You're planning to write what I tell you on paper?

—Yes, sir. I'd like to. Perhaps incorporate some ideas into a novel.

—Then there is no need to pay me. I'll have to go pretty far back. But I can tell you just like I told Eva.

Will nodded, waiting. He didn't mind if Poppy began his story far back at the beginning.

www.ingramcontent.com/pod-product-compliance
Lightning Source LLC
Chambersburg PA
CBHW031109260626
47172CB00001B/292